CLEMENCY BROWNE DREAMS OF GIN

to my family with love

CLEMENCY BROWNE DREAMS OF GIN

Órfhlaith Foyle

ARLEN
HOUSE

Clemency Browne Dreams of Gin

is published in 2014 by
ARLEN HOUSE
42 Grange Abbey Road
Baldoyle
Dublin 13
Ireland
Phone/Fax: 353 86 8207617
Email: arlenhouse@gmail.com
arlenhouse.blogspot.com

Distributed internationally by
SYRACUSE UNIVERSITY PRESS
621 Skytop Road, Suite 110
Syracuse, NY 13244–5290
Phone: 315–443–5534/Fax: 315–443–5545
Email: supress@syr.edu

978–1–85132–109–4, paperback
978–1–85132–110–0, hardback

© Órfhlaith Foyle, 2014

The moral rights of the author have been asserted

Typesetting ┊ Arlen House
Printing ┊ Brunswick Press
Cover art *Clock Tower* and *Dome* by Bernadette Madden
are reproduced by kind permission of the artist,
courtesy of The Kenny Gallery

Clemency Browne Dreams of Gin
has received financial assistance
from the Arts Council under the
Publications/Title by Title Scheme

C

ACKNOWLEDGEMENTS

Thank you to Brendan Barrington for publishing 'Husk' in *The Dublin Review* (2014).

Thank you to John Lavin for publishing 'How I Murdered Lucrezia' in *The Wales Arts Review* (2014).

Thank you to Nuala Ní Chonchúir and Thomas Morris for publishing 'The Suicide Detective' in *The Stinging Fly* (2014).

Thank you to my publisher Alan Hayes at Arlen House for his time, support and great encouragement.

Thank you to Antony Farrell of The Lilliput Press for support over the past years.

A special acknowledgement of the work of Dorothea Tanning (1910–2012), painter, sculptor and writer. Her *Hôtel du Pauvot, Chambre 202* inspired my story 'Soiled Welcome'.

A special thank you to Bernadette Madden for the beautiful cover art from her batik paintings: *Clock Tower* and *Dome*.

CLEMENCY BROWNE DREAMS OF GIN

CLEMENCY BROWNE DREAMS OF GIN

She lights a cigarette and smokes two syllables into the air. Fu-ck. Re-arrange the rhythm. FU-*ck* ... fu-CK.

Her bladder is killing her.

Sitting in this chair in this kitchen with sweat between her legs and her toes, her head swims. She laughs. Almost forty-five and she's drowning in the kitchen. Eye the knife drawer. Practised it before.

She needs some gin.

Fuck.

She walks over to the mirror.

'Clemency Browne', she says out loud.

Fourteen years old again. Running in purple-towelled shorts on a hot afternoon. A dog barks. A car revs in the thick heat joined up by the ice-cream van. Run and running over to the ice-cream man who leans out his head, his large smile ready with rainbow sprinkles.

The pain in her bladder.

Tight, tighter the other boys and girls chanted and she took every one of their pennies for sweets until one night, one boy, one of those older boys who knew what he was capable of reached over and stuck his finger into her belly button and out she whooshed.

A thump sounds from the bedroom above then feet shift towards the bathroom. Clemency shuts down sounds of urination and dreams of her gin.

The bathroom door opens.

It's just the dust off my runners that I have to remember and that brilliant heat so hot it turned my fingers into electricity, and the boy who first loved me, God I loved him ... back, back into his jacket where his ribs were so good.

And the family ... no, don't think of the family ... don't think of all those bits and pieces that made you go wrong ...

The footsteps come down the stairs. It's the smell first. Sweat and body from sleep. Old drink in the skin and a kiss like a razor on her cheek.

Bladder stretching at the smell but screw tight and hard and everything slides down. Easy walk over the black and white kitchen tiles and say the obvious.

'I'm going out for gin'.

Outside the heat lifts up the tar.

'Going without your shoes?' someone yells from the burnt playing field.

She doesn't answer.

He gave her a kid, that boy.

Clemency doesn't want to think.

The air conditioning in the supermarket gives her vertigo. She inherited that from her mother. Don't think. Forget the measurements of family. The mother and father, the three point something of the others. Forget.

Clemency stares at the fruit section for a while.

A kid bumps into her and she smiles at it, watching how it reacts. It waves its hand in front of its face.

'You smell'.

Answer it. 'I don't smell'.

A man makes moo-eyes at all her shiny cents and euros.

Everyone laughs from the vegetable aisle all the way over to the alcohol shelves.

Don't laugh, she calls out in her mind. Jesus, don't laugh.

Her bladder opens. Her urine comes out in a warm stream between her thighs and down to her bare feet.

She stares at the man in front of her.

'I'm Clemency Browne', she says.

Her name sounds useless but she sticks with it.

He leans down, finger-swipes a drop of urine from her foot then puts it close enough to his lips to make Clemency wonder if he's a tender one, but the man flicks his finger over a cabbage crate then says something to her face.

So she presumes he's foreign.

A supermarket employee comes running with a bucket of bleach and a mop. He doesn't hit her feet but he manages to slosh water over her toes and the bleach makes her gag so she pushes towards the drink aisle. Supermarket trolleys avoid her. She tries not to cry. She chooses her gin, pays at the checkout and walks outside.

The sun is so hot she can feel her jeans dry. Her bare toes pick up bits of gravel. She thinks get home and get safe. She focuses on the long cement pathway from the other side of the world, leading past the church to the housing estate. Cars stop once the red light comes. Her gin bottle sits like a baby in her arms. The road shines up as she walks over it. Her shadow wants to run.

Clemency thinks, six days, no maybe three, with make-up on and I can go back there. Her feet pound on the hot cement. Boys playing on the field stop and stare at her as she walks by. One of them copies her. He hunches down and crabs out his legs. He's about eight. She ignores him and continues walking. She reaches a small alley, leans against the wall, lights a cigarette then watches the dead area outside her house. A dog is roasting on the tarmac.

A girl walks by, chubby thighs in shorts and a belly plopping to the tune in her earphones. Eyes slide over Clemency's face. Clemency nods back. Her head hurts. She breathes against the hot and cold feeling in her heart. The girl walks on and the dog looks at Clemency.

She stops at her front door. There is meat frying and a voice on the mobile inside so she sits on the windowsill, opens the bottle of gin, drinks and lights another cigarette.

Fu-ck.

He comes to the door from the kitchen, phone in his hand, desperate to sound harmless and sober.

'Tell your sister I didn't hit you'.

'He didn't hit me', she says into the phone.

Her sister's voice, insistent, younger, sober, completely good.

Get rid of him. Get rid of the drink.

Fu-ck, Clemency smokes.

She hands the phone back. She sucks in more gin. Don't think. Just drink.

Gin slides down to her gut and every thing else slides clear. The old dog belly-bakes in the sun. The ice-cream van turns a semi-circle. Clemency smells herself, raw and filthy in the heat. She closes her eyes and her fourteen-year-old self smiles. Gin jellies her smile, turns it to nothing. Clemency opens her eyes. She squints at nothing. The alley is bright with nothing. The alley is a dead-end dream of nothing.

GOOD MORNING MR TUMNUS

Mr Tumnus. That's what she called him and he wondered why. She was just like he was, one of those forgotten ones suddenly picked up on a jobs scheme and told she was actually worth something again. He liked her hair and her face. Sometimes she walked on the tiptoes of her feet and he liked that. He asked her if she had wanted to be a ballerina when she was young and he stared at her face to see her answer. He wanted to see something sad in her face since she wasn't actually a ballerina, and even though she was still young he could tell she wasn't fresh.

Her answer was so ordinary he could have hit her.

'No', she said. 'I never did'.

She sat down with the others and opened her pot of yogurt.

He liked her shoulders under her thin purple cardigan. He caught a slip-glimpse of her skin there. He smiled and made himself some coffee, then sat down to join in the talk. The talk was about the orientation weekend in Roundstone.

'What happens in Roundstone stays in Roundstone', someone said.

'That's true', someone agreed.

The accents grated. The voices belonged to thick, older women with hanging earrings and large open-viewing cleavages.

He swallowed down coffee then smiled when someone called his name.

'Niall'.

It was the boss woman. Corpulent and swaying on her high heels, and Niall marvelled how such an obese woman could keep her body clean.

'Print these out'.

Print out sheets of paper. File the bastards in order. Use plastic-coated paper clips to bind them. The heat and smell of the printer gave him a good-time feeling. He whistled under his breath. He was good-looking. He had charisma. Women gave him special smiles.

Except for her.

She walked past him now in her ballerina pumps and her heels lifted with each step.

'Hey', he said. 'Why do you call me "Mr Tumnus?"'

She looked at him, her tiptoes still turning as he approached her,

She shrugged and said. 'You look like he walks'.

Her shoulders retreated. It wasn't yet fear but it was something he could almost taste. He held up a photocopied sheet of the hotel accommodation list.

'You're in with Teresa', he said.

She nodded then she spun away towards the welfare office. He stared at her back. She was just like him, wasn't she? One of those damaged people whom the government wanted to keep busy. He had seen her count out her money at the canteen table. She liked dark chocolate and she liked conversation about books and films. She never mentioned men. Some of the older women who had lesbian sides were friendly to her and she was friendly in return but only as far as the dark chocolate conversations at the canteen table.

It was Teresa, who had told him about the Mr Tumnus nickname. She laughed and said Karen had one of those romantic natures that really did nothing but make up dreams and stories.

'Almost lies, really', Teresa considered.

Niall liked the lie. He went home and mentioned it to his wife who looked up from her dinner and said nothing.

Niall wondered who Mr Tumnus really was.

'Just look it up', Teresa told him.

Mr Tumnus wasn't even real. He was made-up out of goat's legs and a little boy chest. He ran around on hooves in the snow and carried parcels tied up in string. He met a young girl under a lamppost and invited her for tea in his cave.

'A Daughter of Eve', Niall mentioned next at the canteen table.

No one really noticed except for Karen, who half-smiled as if she was pleased but Niall did not want to hope too much. He liked the idea that she might be a little afraid, a little wary. He thought of her tiptoes and how they spun. He knew ballerinas had deformed feet.

Mr Tumnus had almost handed his Daughter of Eve over to the White Witch.

Niall watched the film and half-read the book. He played Lucy and Mr Tumnus's scenes on his iPhone. His wife picked up the book and looked at the cover. She saw a strange lion and some children. She didn't see anything else. Niall told her he was considering some adult education. English literature and film studies. She said the book looked weird. He said the lion had some Christ-like tendencies. His wife laughed, stuck some curried beef into her mouth and said wasn't he getting a bit old for an improvement like that?

She told him to mind himself in Roundstone.

He watched the way she dug out her curry from the microwaveable box. Two squares of meat on a fork, dripping green-coloured oil onto her hand, then into her mouth, all that chewing, showing off her cheeks and gaps on the right-hand side of her teeth.

His Daughter of Eve ate hardly ever. He liked that.

He watched the back of her head all the way to Roundstone. He didn't want to sit near her. He just wanted the thought of her. Teresa sat next to him. She said she hated all this orientation idea. It's as if they think we have forgotten how to be human after all our years on the dole, she told him.

She laughed and he laughed.

Karen hadn't been long on the dole but she had gone mentally awry. Niall had zipped her file up on screen and read her history. She was young enough to have done something with her life but she hadn't done much.

Later that night in the hotel's bar the boss woman wobbled her way through the tables and declared that all and sundry must be good. No drunken singsongs, no late night revelry. This was serious EU money they were using. This was the way forward for them all.

She stopped in the middle of the room and looked at every face. For a second, she looked as if she was lying through her smile, but Niall knew they all had to believe her because what else was there to believe.

He nudged Karen's knee with his own.

'You believe in the way forward?' he said.

Teresa snorted but Karen said, 'yes'.

Niall laughed and looked at his pint. After a while, he would start on some whiskey.

'What do you want to be?' he asked her.

Karen reached for her own drink of a small dark red wine, shrugged and said nothing. Tessa snorted at her, picked up some peanuts from a bowl then dribbled them into her mouth.

'It's just life', she said. 'That's all it bloody is'.

She looked around at something else to keep her attention and spotted him in a far corner.

Niall started on some whiskey. He raised it and said, 'here's to Mr Tumnus'.

He put out his legs alongside Karen's stool.

'These aren't goat's legs, are they?'

He put out a hand on her wrist. It was so narrow he could feel bones and blood. On her file it had said 'a psychotic break'. It said she had been a teacher but one day she had walked out, and a week later in her flat she had tried to kill herself with an onion knife.

'I'm going to bed', she told him now.

He watched her disappear into the hotel lobby.

The boss woman started again. She outlined tomorrow's team-building exercises. A part-time professional surfer was going to lead the way and there would be something Celtic on the beach. Stone circles and pagan promises. It would be creative and fun. It would highlight their right temporal lobe according to EU guidelines.

Niall laughed. He was getting drunk.

Later Teresa met him on the stairs. She was going to be busy with his roommate so she handed over the keys to her and Karen's room.

Niall unlocked the door and went inside.

Karen was asleep. He sat on Teresa's bed and waited for a while. He looked at what he could see.

'Karen'.

Slowly, so slowly, she turned and faced him.

She was wearing an ordinary white t-shirt.

Niall thought ballerinas or Daughters of Eve would have worn something more imaginative. He cleared his throat.

'Teresa has found somewhere else'.

He saw her fear. He wanted to keep that fear to himself.

He said, 'it's Mr Tumnus here instead'.

She drew her legs up and stared at him. He moved onto her bed. Her fear was sharp as if shining crystals stood out all over her face.

'I don't want you here', she said.

He moved forward and watched how every crystal on her face seemed to shiver. He tried to kiss them quiet.

'Say "Good Morning Mr Tumnus"', he whispered.

'No', she said.

He put his arm on her shoulders and she tightened. He kept talking about nothing else but her and ballerinas and Daughters of Eve. He kept talking about beauty. He kept holding onto her. He kept expecting love.

He saw something boil inside her eyes. He knew it was hate. He saw it.

She hit him and he fell against the other bed.

She hit him again.

He stared up at her. 'Jesus'.

She stood high and stood hard into the groin.

'Jesus', he squeaked.

She stood back, her foot raised again and ready. She was breathing hard but she was laughing.

'Get out. Get out you stupid, stupid … *man*'.

He got out. He made his way to the bar lounge and he found some left-over whiskey in a small glass at table near the picture window.

He looked into his reflection. It laughed at him.

You stupid, stupid, *man*, it said, you stupid, stupid man.

Cosset's War

Cosset lit his pipe and glanced across at the long velvet green curtains that half-covered the window. He hated conducting business so close to evening. Autumn was almost here and the leaves of the beech tree outside the window were turning a pale and terrible yellow.

He had his afternoon tumbler of watered-down wine in front of him but he had offered his patient only water. The patient's face was red. He was breathing hard and he was thinner than was medically advisable.

Cosset was getting old. Cosset thought of drowning.

When he was a child, Cosset had relished fishing on a lake near his parents' home in Cambridgeshire. His grandfather brought him there. They would sit in the boat and fish. The quiet glass of the lake lay like a door to another universe for the child. He imagined Arthurian ladies hiding their long fingers under stones, waiting for him ... waiting ...

To prevent himself from falling down to them, the child developed a fascination with pond skaters. He fancied he could follow them as he watched their legs flit across the surface of the water.

His grandfather had told him the skater's long legs were slender and wide enough to distribute their body weight over the flow of the lake. Their hind legs were the steering mechanism. The middle legs were for rowing. If the skater were to fall into the water, tiny hairs on its body would trap air into rows of bubbles and pop the skater back onto the surface again.

As long as the child kept his attention on the surface of the water where the skaters flew, he could view the lake as only water – somewhat dangerous but only truly dangerous if you fully submerged your body with the express intention of drowning yourself.

Cosset's patient asked permission to light a cigarette.

He sat forward and his knees, already large enough, loomed into the light. For a second, Cosset could see a human tank in front of him. They *crrr* ... *uuun* ... *cch*, he remembered.

The patient laid his left arm across his knees.

'We don't use shell shock as an excuse any more', Cosset explained.

'They stopped my pension. I was wounded but they stopped it'.

The patient's knees jutted up again, and Cosset tried to imagine the interior of the man's head. The structure of bone followed by the vast sensation of a mind. He thought of the tunnels at Messines.

Cosset had loved the war.

He had loved it like a woman. A terrible, spitting, gut-splaying woman. One you ought to hate, but one that draws you right to her heart, and he had often contemplated a confession ... not to a *padre* of any sort, not even to himself, but once or twice he had managed to find a man in the one of the many mineshafts along the

Messines Ridge, just before detonation, and he had stared at them as if the very wish for his confession could be transferred from his eyes into theirs. He liked these men. He thought of them creeping along the walls of the earth, kicking the clay in front of them while keeping their ears open for German whispers on the other side. Men made into the image of tall and short voles – men made sinewy as weasels.

It was their smell of death mixed with life that Cosset loved the most. The shine in their eyes, the way their clothes gave off the odour of sweat, urine, fear and that sick and dreadful humour that even Cosset wanted to be part of, yet couldn't.

'Come to get lost, sir?'

'Pick out your grave, sir?'

One man tapped his head, then Cosset's. He cramped forward into a static crawl.

'Like that, sir', he instructed him.

The tunnel reminded Cosset of a negative torso. The insides of a woman hollowed from all but the ribs padded with earth. He went down inside her. He mentally spread out his hearing capacity. The men before him and behind him breathed as silent as they could. Their knees pressed onto the hollowed woman's spine. Cosset shut his eyes for a second and apologised to her then he groped forward. His vision bleared in the grisly, greasy yellow light. As if pig's fat was dug into the walls and set to light, smoulder and drip.

Naturally he thought of the tunnel collapsing. The men were used to portraying voles and worms. Their shoulders seemed to change bone structure as they turned corners. Their backsides narrowed down. When they breathed close to him, they stank of rotting teeth.

Once he heard a German speaking on the other side of the wall.

Every man around Cosset shut down his breath.

Beyond the dirt wall, some young man's voice was speaking, very young ... very nearly a girl's tone on its higher register. The man on Cosset's right smiled. He held up one set of fingers and his other thumb. Six hours. He drew his index finger across his throat. Dead in six hours. That young voice in its prospective grave.

Cosset leaned back into the earth wall behind him. He looked beyond the shivering pigskin light and the men's distorted faces.

Sergeant Talbot, he remembered. From Manchester.

'Like a mouse, sir', Talbot whispered into Cosset's ear.

Cosset focussed on the wall in front of him. He imagined he heard the sounds of food being eaten. There was a little singing and as he widened his hearing capacity even more, he thought he could hear the high lone dribbling cry of a descending shell.

Its cry thudded down.

Talbot grinned. 'That's better, sir', he whispered.

Cosset's wine had grown a light scum across its surface. Minute black spots skated there.

Spectacles, Cosset reminded himself. He put them on.

'Any dreams?' he wondered aloud.

'I dream of killing people', the patient answered.

'What sort of people?'

'Men', the patient replied answered. 'Once I tried to kill a woman ... outside a dream ... I had my hands around her neck', the patient pantomimed his throttling technique.

Cosset observed. The patient's fingers clawed around a non-existent throat. Cosset swallowed some wine. The patient's complexion had reddened right to his scalp. His breathing filled the room.

Cosset asked:

'Is she dead?'

The patient relaxed. 'No', he said. 'But I killed my mother's prize hen'.

Cosset glanced at the trees outside the window. In his mind they were like faces and each leaf added to the eyebrows, lips and moustaches.

The patient said, 'you have to cure me'.

Cosset asked, 'why did you kill your mother's hen?'

It seemed such a useless question. For dinner would be the obvious answer. Cosset concentrated on the patient before him. The man was sweating beyond reason. His heels juddered on the floor.

'I don't know', the patient said. He glanced around the room as if he was looking for a way through its walls, but there was just the wallpaper that Cosset's wife had chosen. Purple coloured plums with green vinery and yellow cherubs with pink lips. She said it would give his patients something to look at when they couldn't answer his questions.

Sometimes it's like a game, Cosset once told his wife. *Fixing people's minds.*

Cosset's grandfather had cherished war. He showed the young boy how beautiful a sword was and made it swish through the air as if it had its own voice. Listen to it, his grandfather said. He had killed in the sub-continent with that sword. He jabbed the button-cushioned back of an old chair to show how deep into a body a sword would penetrate. It went right through and his grandson had felt the same thrill go through his own body. He laughed out loud. His grandfather laughed also.

Later when Cosset was older he realised that the blasted old man had been blasted a long time.

He stared at the dark window. He knew it was mutton chops with gravy tonight. The housekeeper never varied Thursday nights. His wife hadn't the heart or the stomach to demand anything else.

You like sheep, Charles. You always did.

He didn't want to go home. He didn't want to listen to her plans for his birthday.

Forty-seven. The number frightened him.

He was younger in the war. The war fed him right.

Cosset asked his patient, 'would you like another biscuit? More water? Or a cigarette?'

The patient began to talk. 'In Jerusalem, I saw a brass face of Jesus Christ. It hung in an Arab shopfront and I just thought ... how silly to have him there ... and I fell in love with a French nun ... only by looking at her ... but I wanted to open her up and climb inside. I imagined her skin would grow over me ...'

Cosset blew slowly through his nose, then he counted his breath back in. He focussed on one cherub on the wall behind the patient's chair.

It was a game, he reminded himself.

The woman, the hen, the French nun and the mother.

Cosset held back a yawn.

Beyond the windowpane the tree's narrow leaves gyrated in the wind. A streetlight began to burn. Also yellow. Cosset shivered. He glanced over at the coat stand. His short silk scarf and thin overcoat hung from one round hook, but Cosset knew that the wind would get him. He thought of his wife. He thought of reaching his front door and finding her in the front room. Her bosom first. He closed his eyes. She hardly allowed him to touch it any more. She complained that it had grown too large because of the children. Once when he told her that he wanted to suckle her also, the responding horror in her face shrivelled him.

She told him that working with people's heads was dangerous for his own. First manage your own thoughts, Charles, she said.

Cosset thought of his grandfather's old head. Bald except for hair circling his ears like a bush scrub. Cosset had held onto those ears. He had held them tight, and the notion of suckling, the temptation to drown had all stemmed from those long moments with his grandfather by the lake's edge. The sound of a pig guzzling, and later, Cosset the child watched his grandfather walk on ahead through the trees towards the family home. He had followed as if nothing had actually happened. He had followed as if his child's penis was still his own, but even the sun knew different, and it paled in the sky, its thin shine failing to burn out the boy's eyes.

Cosset counted his breath then reached for his wine glass. His desk lamp lit up the sugar crystals on the biscuits. He drank his wine and wanted more. He stared at his patient.

'Show me', he ordered.

That evening as he hung up his overcoat in the hallway of his house, Cosset heard his wife twitter in the front room. Guests, he realised. His wife called out his name and he called back a 'yes dear'. He put a smile on his face before he entered and he saw the closed curtains, the gaslight that spotted shadows on the carpet and his wife's friends, all three of them, thin and aging in the same shadow.

Cosset reached for a little round cake the size of a child's eye and popped it in his mouth. It stalled behind his Adam's apple.

He thought of his patient's fingers around that very nub, all that flesh as fragile as transparent bone. The sensation of almost dying, like a warm breath in his ears and under his tongue.

God, he longed for war.

BLESSING

George's sister visited one morning and asked George to fix her television.

'What happened to Larry?' George asked.

Larry had been Blessing's white friend. A tall red-nosed man with effete fingers and a voice that went too high whenever he saw George.

'He is not a good disguise', George's wife said. 'How does she think she fools us all?'

Blessing took a piece of fish from her brother's plate. 'He had to return to England'. Her brother was getting fat and middle-aged. His cheeks looked like a baboon's. Miriam was stuffing him.

'Now you have a new friend', Miriam said.

Blessing addressed her brother. 'There is no picture. Tabby says it should go back to the shop but I said you are a genius of electricity'.

After they had got married Miriam said to George that Blessing was wrongly made.

'She admires my body', she complained.

George said that Blessing had an artistic eye for detail.

Miriam laughed at him. They were sitting in her father's car. It was hot and his cologne mixed with the smell of the leatherette seats. He felt that Miriam was sitting too close. He was burning beside her.

Blessing had warned, 'don't do it, my brother'.

He looked at her now from his side of the table and he said, 'Blessing ... be careful'.

He was her brother. He could afford to be direct. He smiled beyond her head and onto the opposite wall. His wedding photo was there. His parents. His wife. His sister. His wife had been pregnant. The wedding had been fast.

At the feast Blessing had stirred tongues by dancing too close with a woman. Their father beat her that night and Blessing left the house the next day. She took one suitcase and her driving licence. She worked her way through university. She never said how she got the money. George knew stories about that. He read the newspaper and listened to church services about men and women who sold same-sex favours for money. He knew someone like that in a bar. A small man with a big smile who bought everyone drinks all the time. He did things with men and George tried so hard not to be curious.

Blessing said, 'Miriam, you are a good cook. My brother is fat and happy'.

Miriam said nothing but she thought I would like that smile dragged from your face.

Blessing tapped her fingers on the table.

'George ... you eat too slow'.

He wiped his mouth. He wondered how he was supposed to fix her television. He wasn't good with wires anymore. He hardly remembered the colour of the earth wire or the neutral one. Plugs had long ago defeated him. Miriam said he was too lazy to complete simple home repairs. She had expected any man she married to have a good working knowledge of family duties. He had failed.

Now Miriam said, 'it's George's day off'.

His sister shrugged, 'just a look and you can meet Tabitha'.

'I saw her', Miriam said. 'Small and dumpy … I thought you liked tall girls, like me'.

Blessing stood up. 'George', she said.

George talked as he got ready. 'This is my day-off. We are taking the children to the park. We are shopping. This is a very busy day. A broken television is not important'.

Outside he looked up the length of the street towards Mombasa Road. 'Did you walk?'

'Taxi'.

They got into George's car.

'Tabitha likes to watch television', Blessing said.

'What about your lap-top?'

'She likes television'.

George stared at his sister. She had always been certain. She had always been powerful.

Tabitha was sitting in front of the television. She threw up her hands when she saw Blessing and George.

'Blank. It is still blank'.

'So no miracle?' George tried to joke.

Tabitha stood up to shake his hand. Blessing smiled at them both. 'I'll get some beers'.

'It is only 9.30', George said. But he wanted a beer to cool down his head. He was afraid of the television. It looked new. It looked as if it should work on its own. He hunkered down in front of the screen.

Both he and Tabitha took their beers.

Cheap Indian beer, George thought. He looked at the bottom expecting to see a cockroach.

Tabitha got close to him. He could see the side of her eye's pupil. She smelled ordinary, nothing special. Even Larry had been an ordinary disguise. All beige safari shirts and Ray-Bans with desert boots. He had hardly ventured outside the safer parts of Nairobi but Blessing brought him to parties and made it worth his while to act as her boyfriend.

Their father swallowed his disgust. At least it was male, he said. Their mother prayed with their church.

Tabitha grinned at George. 'I bet you cannot fix this'.

She sounded like a teacher.

'It's just wires', Blessing said.

Tabitha swivelled on her heels. 'Blessing, you are *too* optimistic'.

George smiled. 'I can fix this'.

Tabitha snorted. She pointed at her vague reflection in the TV. 'Just grey noise, and I know you cannot fix this'.

George got behind the television and opened it up within fifteen minutes. He looked at its insides.

'It's still plugged in', Tabitha said.

She laughed at the idea of his possible electrocution.

George unplugged the TV. 'It's LED', he said.

Tabitha laughed. 'You see Bless? I knew he would fail'.

George stared at the lights and the microchips that faced him. He told the truth. 'This is not good', he said.

Blessing sat on the edge of her settee. She rolled some beer in her mouth then swallowed, then said. 'It might be the tuning'.

George stared at her.

'It's just out of the box', Tabitha explained.

George closed up his mouth. 'False pretences', he accused Blessing.

Blessing laughed. 'Oh relax brother. You needed to get away from Miriam and Tabitha wanted to see you'.

'Yes I did', Tabitha said. She pushed her body into the settee and placed a hand on Blessing's knee. 'Three children', she marvelled.

'Beautiful children', Blessing said.

Tabitha nodded at the television. 'You *can* tune it in, can't you, George?'

George followed the instructions and tuned it in. They settled on a programme on night-time Nairobi.

'It's not Sydney', Tabitha said.

'Tabitha is a flight attendant'.

George said, 'you sound like a teacher'.

Tabitha turned her mouth down. Blessing laughed and kissed her.

It was an ordinary kiss. It wasn't even on the lips.

'Your brother is watching'.

'He's just curious'.

'Yes', George said, brave with beer. 'I'm just curious'.

He didn't say much more for the next hour because Tabitha kept talking about the party she was planning for later that day. It would be lunch and music followed by more food, drink and music. Finally she asked George for money.

'Your sister says you have American Express'.

'I am going to the park with my children', he told her.

She smiled and shook her head. 'You have to party with us'.

Guests began to arrive. They brought peppered chicken, cooked fish, rice and beans, roasted goat and Tusker beer. They shook George's hand. The kitchen table was laid out with food. Blessing danced with Tabitha and someone else. George watched their hips slide, dip and shake.

George hid in the bathroom and rang Miriam from his mobile.

She was angry. 'The children are crying because we are not in the park'.

'It is a big television, Miriam'.

'You cannot fix anything here, George. How can you fix something for your sister and her devil whore?'

'She is not a devil and she cannot be a whore if she is with my sister'.

George heard Miriam suck in her breath. 'Maybe this is what you want'.

George said nothing.

'Maybe you are happy there', Miriam said.

'I am happy with you', George told her.

He went back outside to the party and looked for Blessing. She was sitting with a group of them around an iced bag of beers. She called over and he came, lifting his sandaled feet over bare knees or trouser legs and beautiful Italian leather shoes. A man touched his shoulder. Blessing said, 'that is my married brother'.

The man who had touched him lifted back his fingers. '*Eeeeh*', he said and flicked his hand over the ice bag.

'He fixes TVs very well', Tabitha announced from behind George. She kissed his head. 'Brother-in-law', she said.

The conversation limped between smiles and George chose another beer. Someone handed him a plate of chickpeas and a small fish that looked as if it had been boiled too long in milk. He said thank you and began to eat. The conversations were very normal. No one talked about evil things. No one mentioned if they went out hunting for little boys or girls to have sex with and so turn them into tiny demons.

So George told a story. He wanted to prove to Blessing and to her friends and to Teacher Tabitha that he was harmless to them. He understood them. He said, 'I used to drink in a bar'.

Someone laughed. 'Not any more?'

Blessing said, 'his wife doesn't like men who smell of beer'.

The laughter made George happy. He continued, 'in the bar was a man just like you'.

'Like who?' Blessing said.

A small silence but a polite silence and George knew that everything he was going to say would sound all right because he would make it sound right.

George stretched his arm out to the group then pointed at his sister. 'Like you, only male'.

'I'll bet', Tabitha said.

'Everyone knew what he did', George said and then he stopped. He had to choose his words well. He wanted to show he meant no harm.

'So what happened?' Tabitha said.

George shrugged. 'He was just a happy man'.

'What was his name?'

George stuffed a spoonful of chickpeas in his mouth. 'Jonathan'.

Blessing opened her eyes wide.

'That was his name', George told her. 'I think he was an engineer'.

Blessing's guests looked at each other, then they looked at George.

George nodded over at the music group Tabitha had rustled up. 'Good music, Tabby', he said.

Blessing said, 'only I call her Tabby'.

'What did you do to Jonathan?' Tabitha said.

'Me? I did nothing. I liked Jonathan'.

He drank more beer just to stop him from seeing Jonathan's face.

'You beat him, didn't you?'

George shook his head.

He knew he had not beaten Jonathan. He had just heard the screams.

'You beat him', Tabitha said.

32

'You would do that to me', his sister said.

'No', he told them both.

He glanced around at the other men. Smooth looking men in cool shirts and trousers. Their shoe leather shone. Their ties sparkled with false gems.

'I wouldn't do anything', he told them.

They put back their heads and smiled as if they believed him. They told him to have some more beer.

Blessing sat on Tabitha's knee and Tabitha's arms fastened around the breast section of Blessing's dress. George chewed his meal and tried not to think of Jonathan's mouth.

Women reminded George of chickens. Their flesh had a flat taste. You needed to spice it up, and that was why George had chosen angular Miriam as his safe wife and he focussed on a bone in her shoulder or the almost straight line of her hip and he wished up a man instead, a man like Jonathan.

Blessing said, 'have some more beer, brother'.

George studied the multi-coloured lights that Tabitha had trailed from the back door of Blessing's house and around the surrounding fence. He stared at the barbecue smoke and at the melting ice. He stared at the dancing men and women. He stared at Blessing kissing Tabitha. He focussed on their same hands and same thighs and on their same female lips.

How do they do it, George wondered. How do they love?

CONVERSATION IS NOT YOUR ENEMY

The prison counsellor advised her to do something ordinary.

'Like what?'

'Buy a coffee. It'll get you used to real people again'.

And later the truck driver asked, 'where are you off to, love?'

He had manners. He said, 'excuse me', as he shifted gears. He also avoided looking at her knees, her hands and sometimes her face.

Although Judith knew that he liked her face.

A plum-coloured lipstick lifted from a pharmacy in Temple Bar had lifted her cheeks, and a tube of mascara from a supermarket had made her eyes look good while she sat in the truck's passenger seat and watched all the small people outside move about in their lives. Small people with their shopping bags full of Christmas paper and tinsel.

Judith lit another cigarette and watched a woman get out of the passenger side of another parked truck.

A young girl really, already tossed about by the driver and now he took her hand, then her shoulders and rammed her close into his side. An ok man by the looks of him, Judith thought. His truck had Spanish writing on it.

Her driver was Irish but heading into Poland.

'Ever been there?' he had asked her soon after he had picked her up.

'No'.

'Ever outside Ireland at all?'

'No', she was just going to say again but then she remembered her counsellor's instruction. 'Conversation is not your enemy. Words are your friends'.

'No, never outside Ireland', Judith managed to elaborate.

'I love getting out of Ireland', the driver said. He focussed on the ice-rain on his windscreen. 'I hate what they have done to the place, don't you?' He looked at her expecting an answer. She didn't know how to answer. She had been gone for ten years. She had seen everything happen on the TV.

'Where are you off to?'

'Travelling', she said.

He watched her take out her smokes. He said he didn't mind and she felt he did, but she smoked anyway, blowing out her open window while he fiddled with the radio stations. He liked French rap music.

His head bounced on his neck as he drove the truck onto the motorway. The speed limit flashed in Judith's eyes. She breathed in the speed and felt her mind rush on ahead. It left a black space inside her head.

Her mother had come to see her the week before.

'We can't have you back, Judith'.

'Conversation'. The counsellor's voice squeaked inside Judith's head. 'Persist through harmless words. Say "hello" and "how are you?" If there is no uptake, say "goodbye" or "see you". It's simple if you start simple'.

'I love you Mam'.

'He'd be nearly ten years old now', her mother said.

The truck driver was polite.

'Have you any kids?'

His head was still bouncing to French rap and the road in front of the windscreen was like a straight dive to nowhere.

'No'.

He glanced at her, smiled in a mild-man way, and said, 'didn't think you looked old enough for kids'.

It was a nice lie. It made her relax and consider her future.

She had this idea of being real. Either in London where the language was more or less the same, or in France, where she could ape their vowels and mop up kitchen floors for a while and she could watch people. She could study how they handled each other, how they spoke and looked at each other, since she hadn't really ever mastered that trick.

'What's Poland like?' she asked her truck driver.

Even his fingernails were polite. They barely grazed the edge of her skirt.

'Poland's fine', he said. He looked out of the window at the darkened sky.

'Are you hungry?'

It was one of those massive truck diners. It had a neon cowboy on one side of its roof and a leprechaun on the other.

'I'll finish my cigarette', Judith told him. He glanced back once or twice and she waved her cigarette smoke towards him. Once he was gone, she tuned into a local radio station and listened to the voices as if she was learning words again. She sat back and closed her eyes, not wanting to think. It would be nice, she thought, not to wake up. She never had the nerve but she used to daydream of somehow being killed by a run-away car; not caring, and not doing anything about it, but just wanting that dark, lovely space to keep her safe and warm and dead.

There was a noise so Judith opened her eyes. She was cold. Snow was expected. There was always snow on this side of Ireland. In prison she used to watch the Guinness television ad for snow. She loved how warm it made her feel. She imagined that she was the woman of the couple who had friends over for drinks. They lived in one of those old-fashioned Dublin houses. The snow was coming down, Christmas lights were bright and the woman leaned into her husband or whatever he was and they waved their friends goodbye and goodnight, and everything seemed so good and lovely.

Now she watched the young girl being manhandled over to the truck diner. The girl's shoes skittered on the iced tarmac. The driver held her up by her jacket collar. He laughed. She laughed.

Judith threw out her cigarette, rolled up her window and jumped out of the truck. The cold air bit her face. The counsellor had warned her about the weather. Worse winter for years he had heard. He was afraid the dark light would affect her mind and her thoughts. She had said no, it wouldn't. It never had. Her thoughts had always been the same. He had sat there, a milky-man pudding. A person changes, he had promised her. A person grows.

Judith halted in the shadow of the diner door. She could smell oil and chips. The driver had said she could order anything she liked. He had glanced at her legs in their black tights. He said he wouldn't be surprised if she was into salads.

Judith entered the diner. She saw roast beef and pork. If she had a good dinner, she knew she'd have to pay for it in some way.

Heads turned to look at her. Judith had always looked good walking. Her legs still had the shape of a fifteen year old. Her skirt was a Marks and Spencer's tweed but her jumper was pink cashmere. Both were from a St Vincent de Paul shop.

The truck driver pulled out a chair for her. She remembered his name as soon as she sat down.

'Thank you Benny'.

Did she lock the passenger door he wondered and she said she did, but she knew she couldn't remember. She tossed her hair and looked around for the girl who was now seated with three men. The girl saw Judith.

Well, you asked for it, Judith silently informed her.

Then she concentrated on Benny.

'Benny', she said.

He smiled and offered to get her food.

'They have Yorkshire pudding', he suggested.

While he was gone, she looked out of the window. Snow was starting. Flakes of it collected on the tarmac outside. It looked so innocent. She wondered how they had decided snow was innocent and she was not.

They had had to decide if it had been wilful neglect or wilful murder. She thought she could have told them either one but her legal aid told her to stay quiet. He had told her that with the psychiatrist's report there was always a chance she was somehow innocent.

So sometimes she had to remind herself that she had been a mother once.

She had not wanted it but there it was in its cot, in its clothes. She had stared at it for a long time. Her mother had cooed over it. Her boyfriend had said, well now, you've got what you've wanted all along.

But she had not wanted it. And it was alive. Something alive that she had never wanted. She called it what? She called it Aaron after her boyfriend.

They called it 'Baby Z'. She had laughed when she heard that 'Z' for the end. Her boyfriend told the newspapers he would have saved 'Z' if he had known what was in Judith's mind, but he had left her by then. He was innocent, he said. He loved that baby. His son, he remembered to call it in later newspaper reports. His son.

The psychiatrist's report said it was a possible break from reality.

Benny returned with the food. Judith picked up her knife and fork and began to eat. The food tasted ordinary. Conversation, she remembered.

'I lied before', she said, chewing meat while reaching for water.

Benny stopped eating. 'What?'

'I had one baby once'.

'Oh', Ben said.

'A cot death'.

The counsellor had told her that she couldn't use that excuse anymore. The truth was that she had let it starve. She remembered walking down the hallway of her flat, dressed for work, and knowing that the baby was in its room, in its cot, growing quieter as days went by. Sometimes she listened. Sometimes she knew she was doing wrong. Other times she didn't mind.

'One of my sons died in a car accident', Benny said after a while.

'I'm sorry', Judith replied. She studied his sad face then consciously drooped the corners of her own mouth.

Benny smiled at her.

I'm doing well, she realised.

It was post partum depression, her legal aid had said. It was sociopathic, the prosecution said, and Judith had listened to them all and she had tried hard to decide which one had to be right. As hard as she had tried to love the baby but then she stopped feeding the baby, then she forgot the baby little by little.

It had been so easy.

Benny was wiping his eyes. 'I still cry', he explained.

The counsellor had said, 'conversation is not your enemy'.

'Aaron', Judith said out loud. A flash of his small face on its pillow, the sound of her own breathing, and his little body all curled and messed up with the blanket.

It took Benny seconds to realise what Judith meant.

'Conor', he reciprocated.

Judith looked out the window again.

'Snow', she said and prodded the handle of her knife at the white tarmac.

Benny nodded. 'I like you', he said, without looking at her.

Judith took a drink of water. She blinked at the light on Benny's half-turned face. She breathed normally. The lights in the place were normal. The snow thickly hefting through the air outside was also normal and now in a way, in this moment, she was normal.

THE SUICIDE DETECTIVE

His office was on the third floor of a building in Dublin city.

I sat down on the other side of his desk. He handed me a notebook and said, 'please write his particulars there'.

I wrote down my brother's name. He had been dead for six weeks. Most nights I woke up wondering how does a body decompose within that time? He had been a nurse. I used to love the way he was so gentle with hurt people, as if they were animals that he couldn't help loving.

The Suicide Detective's name was Leon and I had heard about him from a mourner at the funeral.

'He doesn't do anything illegal', she insisted, 'except make up a future for your dead loved one from the clues you give him'.

It was a strange thing to do. But I wanted to be strange for a while.

I held the handwritten pages of my brother's past and his leftover future.

Joseph, aged 16, brought a near dead cat home and nursed it back to life.

That bit was true. I had watched him place his delicate fingers on the cat's torn legs and on the edges of its worm congested gut. My brother had some sort of love in him passed down from a dead ancestor of ours. One of those mad ones whose lives were short and never really there anyway.

Joseph, aged 27, had a sudden re-occurrence of childhood melancholy after job loss then wife loss.

I skipped that part. I went onto the made-up end.

'It's like a prayer what he does', the mourner had purred at me.

My brother woke up. My brother sat for a long time and listened to the air inside his room. He remembered that he had a twin sister, plus others and a family that loved him. He remembered the cat. He remembered the first dead human body he had ever seen.

Then he made some cocoa like in the old days. Then he rang me. Then I came.

'Consider it an inverse Gestalt practise', Leon said.

I stared at his clear handwriting then I stared at his office walls and floor. They were dirty. The room was very cold. A spider crawled along my in-step, up my calf and turned about on my knee.

My mother crawled into the bath and she did not come out for a month. My father continued to work yet he was shrinking every day. My siblings did normal things to survive. I burrowed next to anyone I could find.

So I kissed Leon's cheek.

'Ooops', he said. Then he smiled from the corners of his mouth.

His sheets were very clean, and he was very warm, and I burrowed deep.

ALICE GROWS UP

There was a well-frosted collection of some scattered dog shit and an old drinking bowl scuffed and dinged. The bowl contained stagnated water and a drowned worm.

A voice shouted 'ALICE'.

Alice bent and lifted the worm out of the dog bowl and laid it on the stone ground.

'Alice!'

Alice looked up.

Gerry was leaning out the top left-hand corner of the old house. Her left, she corrected, as Gerry would have corrected.

'Come inside Alice', Gerry said.

Alice shook her coat free of yard debris and as she walked, she noticed thin splashes of dark dirt, black and haphazard over the yard.

Gerry swung the back door open and introduced the kitchen to her. The table and the chairs, the hot tea flask, which was open and steaming, and the packet of Kimberley biscuits he had bought on the way here.

'Your favourite', he reminded her.

Not really, she thought, and chose the chair nearest to the kitchen's back door.

'The trees are full of crows', she told him. 'And I think there was a dog here once'.

'Yeah, they got the dog too', he said.

Alice ate one of the biscuits as an adult would eat it, neat bites of ginger and sugared marshmallow that stung her gums and clogged her throat.

He said, 'I made the bed upstairs'.

Alice picked another biscuit.

She said, 'maybe not today, Gerry'. Like a grown-up woman says it or like something she had heard on TV.

Just a second went by. Gerry smiled then said, 'ok'.

He leaned back in his chair to look out onto the yard.

'Bits of the blood still on the yard out there'.

Alice's mug of tea was heavy-bottomed and a man's name was painted blue about its belly. Michael, she read.

'Guess where they found the dog?'

Gerry didn't wait for Alice to guess.

'Drowned in the rainwater barrel with a rope round its neck', he said.

It had been Gerry's idea to come here. He liked visiting places that had been in the news. He liked impromptu picnics as well. He believed he was an explorer of events.

Only once had they done it in his house. That place was full of pictures of his wife and his children, and Alice had seen them for real in the local supermarket. They all had his hair, even his wife, and while his wife stood at the checkout watching all her bright-green vegetables skim over the scanner, Gerry had watched Alice in the next line wrestle with boxes of cheap washing powder and butter fudge.

She remembered feeling the blush boil in her face and her heart went hard in her chest, while in between her legs she felt something slick and cold.

Gerry said, 'they killed the old woman first'.

Alice imagined the dead old woman drinking out of her cup, sitting down for her breakfast, chatting to her husband about the day or about shooting the crows from the trees. Alice heard Gerry say, 'the old guy was dragged into the yard then left to die in the cold'.

Alice looked beyond Gerry to the other doorway that led to a tiny hall, then a stairs, then a landing, then a room, and then a bed. Her parents thought she was just being a teenager these days. The secretive sort but not so remote a teenager that they worried. Alice had been vigilant about that. She still laughed and carried on at home, but inside she felt as if something sick was growing inside her.

Gerry had varicose veins on his legs, and sometimes he farted as he slept.

Gerry was her father's colleague. He taught geography and first step philosophy for the fifth years. He liked throwing out questions of a utilitarian nature. He said people had to think their way through life. He said the new and improved Ireland needed thinkers like him. He said once religion was ground head down into the dirt, then those who could fashion great unspeakable thoughts could create a better world.

Sometimes he reminded Alice of a dictator in a classroom, rambling about some new world that really had nothing to do with her. Some of the other girls in the class said he'd be worth the ride if they ever got the chance. They liked the way he smelled when he bent down to look at their work.

Gerry said the trouble with this useless country was that no one thought how to make it clean. He liked being clean. After sex with her he used baby wipes all over his body and then he used them all over her.

Yet Alice had her own thoughts.

Alice liked to imagine her thoughts sliding out of her brain and into the world. Sometimes when she closed her eyes she could feel her thoughts spread and grow into pictures, so real it made her blood fast-forward.

Alice wanted the dead dog to come barking into the house. Her head was too full of Gerry. Her nose was sick of his smell.

He shoved a whole Kimberley biscuit into his mouth then chewed out crumbs. 'You think too much', he said about her silence.

In the car on the way to the house Alice had watched Gerry switch his jeep's gears and run the steering wheel through his fingers. He was talking all the time, excited that they would have the place to themselves. She wriggled her toes in her boots. Ice water had got in and her socks had frozen onto her feet.

He was talking and she just let his talk wander inside her head.

A group of men had invaded the old couple's home looking for money. It was pension day and as everyone knew old people in the country had never really trusted the banks in the first place and so stuffed money under mattresses or in holes behind the skirting boards. The men went through their house then went through their dog.

'It must have howled to death before it drowned', Gerry observed.

In one philosophy class, Gerry had said that people came together because their minds met on an invisible level. It can be a good meeting or it can be a bad one. That's why there are bullies and victims. That's why there is love and hate. That's why the old couple were chosen to die, and that's why Gerry chose Alice.

She had dropped her sandwich in front of his shoe in the canteen.

He smiled and said, 'you're Peter Mahon's daughter, aren't you?'

He bought her a yogurt for dessert. He mentioned that she had an enquiring mind. He said he noticed that she read a lot. He was impressed.

No one saw anything. No one.

Gerry said 'let's keep it a secret', and even though she was old enough to know that hardly ever worked, Alice wanted the secret. She wanted to be special. Gerry said that was the ultimate consequence of being the middle child.

The first time was dark, hard and stuffy in the back of his car parked in the grounds of an abandoned housing estate, and afterwards she and he wandered in and out of the houses, kicking rubble, examining once newly-installed toilets now turned brown, and built-in wardrobes that had only ever housed bats instead of clothes, and Alice poked her finger into an old swallow's nest in a bedroom, wondering aloud at how soft it had been there for the chicks.

She knew she sounded dreamy.

Gerry told her he loved her then.

She wondered if she should believe him.

She stood back and let him rub her face clean of whatever was still on it, her rose colour lip balm, her mother's foundation, her own silver metallic eye shadow. Gerry dug the last bits of balm from the corners of Alice's mouth. 'You look better younger', he decided.

In the beginning Alice had liked being chosen by Gerry. She had liked the way he said her name. Once he said he'd like to get into her mind and see how it worked, and while she lay on his bed, she contemplated the shadows on Gerry's bedroom ceiling. The shadows looked like grey worms. Her stomach curled whenever Gerry kissed her. His hair was going white behind his ears. He said he'd paint her portrait one day. She knew this was a lie. She knew all this as he lay on top of her whispering about her adult mind in a girl's body.

He said the middle female child of most families had a secret life that no one could ever guess. He said secrets were good. He said after all she was seventeen and she had a right to her own secrets.

'They tortured the old woman', Gerry told her.

Alice thought of the old man drinking his own tea. She thought of him sitting in his old jumper and she thought of the dog sniffing at the old man's boots, and the small quiet ticking sound his watch might have made on his wrist.

'They found cigarette burns on her', Gerry said. 'She must have screamed', he marvelled.

Alice had never heard a real old woman scream. She imagined it now and it sounded white inside her head. She imagined the old woman's mouth stretched wide so that her gums shone and her tongue stuck hard into the air. Alice named her Sybille. Gerry picked up biscuit crumbs on his fingers. Alice drank some more tea.

'They lived out here', Gerry continued. 'In a way, they asked for it, didn't they? Guards' station gone and it's now rich pickings on the savannah'.

He was making a philosophical reasoning of the situation.

After all, you're seventeen, aren't you?

We're not doing anything immoral, are we?

It's love, isn't it?

He had always expected a 'yes' answer and Alice always gave it, yet something had gone funny inside her recently. At first she thought it could have been the beginnings of a baby, but that hadn't happened.

Gerry smiled at her. 'Let's head upstairs'.

The bedroom was cold and the window was open. The crows stared out from the trees.

'Michael could have shot them from here', Alice said.

Gerry looked up from undressing himself. He looked funny, big and half-naked in the corner underneath a sideways crucifix fastened to the wall above him.

'Who?'

'Michael. The man who died here'.

'Take off your clothes', Gerry said.

He preferred Alice to start undressing from the bottom up.

'I don't want to do it here. They'll watch'.

'Who?'

'The crows'.

Gerry's belly poofed out over his penis.

'Don't be stupid Alice'.

According to Gerry, stupid people filled the earth with tiny thoughts and useless action. Stupid people believed in God. Stupid people defied rationality and reason. Only stupid people chose other stupid people.

Alice knew she wasn't stupid. But she was having sex with an old man and she didn't like it anymore. It didn't feel like a sin but it felt wrong anyway.

In the beginning Gerry had seemed cuddly, like an Irish version of Einstein. He had a way of breaking the heads of his pencils with his thumb. He only ever wrote corrections in pencil. He said if any student rubbed out a comment they didn't like, then that was their decision to live with their stupidity.

Alice balanced back on her heels. She felt her mind open wide inside her head and she felt her blood ease into every part of her. She knew she couldn't bring Michael and Sybille back from the dead but she could imagine their faces. She could imagine all their actions of the day before they died. She imagined that they loved each other.

Not like Gerry said he loved her.

Not that slick cold feel of him inside her. Not that kiss he gave his wife outside the supermarket and the way he held his wife's neck while she tried to put the groceries in the back of the jeep. Not even her parents' love which was dulled down into filling the dishwasher and watching the TV.

'Alice', Gerry said. 'Alice, take off your clothes. We haven't got all day'.

Michael turned from the window and aimed his gun at Gerry.

Shoot him, Alice thought. Michael fired and although Gerry did not fall down dead, Alice still felt something happy rise inside her.

She walked out of the room and went back down the stairs and into the kitchen. She saw Sybille call to the dog, something like *Jack* or *Lucy*, and Alice saw other things as well. She saw the night when men came into the house, men who burned Sybille's arms and legs; men who spat into her eyes while her husband sat tied to the chair, and Alice followed one of the men who went outside for the dog, called to him, grabbed him, then drowned him in the water barrel; and all this time Alice had been in bed somewhere with Gerry, feeling his skin on her, feeling his breath, his hair, and his toe-nails grating on her shins.

On the television news, everyone said that the old couple were no harm to anyone. Alice remembered watching the coffins coming out of the door. She remembered listening to people talk to the camera about how the country was swimming in its own pus of violence and murder.

'Innocents are being slaughtered', someone said.

Alice's mother said, 'anyone would think we've dived back into the Middle Ages'.

Alice's father said, 'the country is eating itself'.

He stuck a rasher on his fork. Alice watched him chew. Her father chewed in a different way to Gerry. Her father was more relaxed. He was polite and he didn't allow anything to fall out of his mouth. He smiled at Alice once he finished chewing.

He said, 'what's up doc?' His old joke that he used to use on her when she was younger, and she had smiled back and said 'nothing, Bugs'.

Alice swallowed back ginger and marshmallow bile. Sybille smiled at her from the window. She stood there, her arms resting on the edge of her sink while her heels slid over the backs of her old shoes. Alice stared at her until she could see every grain in the old woman's skin, every freckle, every piece of old, grey hair that dropped back in long waves from her head.

Alice looked about at the Kimberley biscuit crumbs on the table. Then she stared at the chairs and imagined the murderers sitting in them, picking up bits of crumb on their fingers. Maybe they were nice to begin with; maybe they looked for directions or offered to fix the gutters or jet stream the yard.

Missus, we don't charge much.

Sir, will you mind that dog from my ankles?

Gerry came into the kitchen. He was ready to be nice.

'We'll go somewhere else', he said.

Alice walked out into the yard and stood there to stare at the dark stains of blood. Michael would have crumbled down, she thought. He would have seen the men's boots come down on his head. She thought of him crying for Sybille.

She felt her thoughts run towards her feet, and she imagined herself backwards; back into the canteen where this time her sandwich never fell. It lay on its small plate until she sat down next to one of her friends, and Gerry walked past, still the nice version of Einstein.

She thought, *I'll go back and be the same again*.

She remembered that she had been two days from seventeen the first time. An early starter, Gerry had joked and his eyes shone on her skin in the back of his jeep. There was his smell and the sliding feel of his smile.

'Alice'. He was in the jeep now, twisting the key, moving the windscreen wipers.

She shivered a little in her coat and she looked down at the small curving road beyond the old farm.

'I'll walk', she said.

He laughed, glanced through the windscreen, then reached his free hand out to her through the open passenger door.

'Don't be stupid'.

'I'll walk'.

He laughed again. Uncertain but still like a teacher in the classroom.

'Get in, Alice, for god's sake'.

She stared at him. He couldn't see inside her. No one could. Her thoughts were so wide now they drew a line through the trees and the crows flew and cawed away into the sky. She imagined her parents in front of the TV with Saturday night take-away on their laps and her sisters and brothers in various rooms doing small and secret various things.

And she thought of Michael and Sybille's deaths. Small, tiny and alone deaths with men laughing above them, and the remaining ginger and marshmallow revolted in her gut, then dribbled through her lips; and she thought of Gerry inside her, beside her and on her, and she saw it all now because she had never seen it before.

ELSJE CHRISTIAENS HANGING ON A GIBBET

The boatman rowed me out to Volewijck moor to see the dead.

'I might not wait for you', he warned so I paid him well.

The dead were fastened onto prangers and gallows.

'Like a forest, eh?' the boatman said. He sat back onto the edge of his boat, lit his pipe, then gestured at a body to the left of us.

It hung from a medium-sized gallows. It was male and its breeches hung loose from its hips.

'That is Daniël', the boatman said. 'He killed his wife'.

I stepped onto the marsh and a tiny spring bird of grey colour lifted from the reeds. The boatman whistled through his lips and the bird flew upwards into the orange sky.

The dead man's odour was the ripe odour of meat. His head had peeled away from its neck to reveal the small yellowing tips of his spine.

The boatman's voice hummed on the breeze.

'Will Daniël satisfy, master?'

'No', I answered.

The boatman laughed. 'Well, there is plenty'.

I glanced across Volewijck moor.

'It is today's execution that I want to see', I told the boatman.

He nodded and screwed up his eyes. 'You can tell the fresh ones because their heads are higher than the others', he said.

I screwed my eyes as well and a head or two seemed clearer to me. Strands of hair and strands of clothes and as I walked further into the field, I saw how silent the world is when we are dead.

Today's execution was of an eighteen year old girl.

She had hit her landlady with an axe and the old woman fell into the cellar and to her death. The baker had said to me, 'what do you expect from an immigrant, and one from Denmark?' He said he knew the landlady to be a business sort. The girl was not paying for her room. The landlady demanded payment.

'And the Danish bitch replied with an axe'.

He looked at me. 'Are you paying the bill today, Master Rembrandt?'

'My son does not trust me', I said.

He laughed before I did. I was never good with money. What I bought with money made me happy. It made my Saskia happy. I made her happy yet we hardly made children, except for Titus.

And Titus did not like death.

'Why not draw one of the girls in the market, father? A fish girl or an apple girl; a living girl'.

The Danish girl had shown no remorse.

An axe, I thought and I looked for that among the more recent dead.

Grey sludge sucked at my boots. Birds watched me.

She had shown no remorse. She had stood before the stuffed rich men of Amsterdam and said nothing. Her clothes were still bloody. Her crime was so visible they were amazed at her silence. She was 'not permitted the earth', the rich in judgement said. Her body was to be hung with the axe until the winds and birds devoured her, they said. They garrotted her outside the Town Hall in Dam Square.

I found her body at the northern end of the gallows field.

She was tied onto the pranger. Her feet were encased in little boots. Her head fell a little into her right shoulder and her right arm was held shorter than her left. She looked like a child ready to be embraced. If she was alive I could have put my hands under her arms and lifted her down.

Her eyes were closed.

The axe hung from the wood on her left side.

I began to draw.

Elsje's small head was lodged between the arms of the pranger and her eyelids were etched onto the blue white of her face. Titus said, what did she expect of us? How could she think we would have been merciful?

There was no decay except that her hair seemed thin above her forehead and her fingertips were dark. I moved closer. Her eyelashes were long, her mouth latched sideways on her face. It is hard to draw innocence, but a pen can do it well and you must leave space for the flesh to plump and fill with light.

'Ah, you found her'.

It was the boatman.

'The boat?' I asked.

'Safe, safe', he said as he walked around Elsje.

He was getting tired waiting. He said if I paid another few *dalders* he would be honoured to wait as long as I needed to stay.

I paid him and I waited until his pipe smoke disappeared at the edge of the marsh before I returned to my work.

Titus had said, 'be careful not to breathe so close to her'.

He was afraid that the plague lay in wait in rotting bodies. He had watched his stepmother Hendrickje die infested with boils. The boils turned black and the yellow oozed out. She saw me watching her. *Do not paint me like this.*

After she died I painted her as Juno.

I drew Elsje from the side. The axe hung parallel to her breast. A bird flitted onto the rope that bound her legs and burrowed its beak in the stuff of her dress. Marsh water seeped into my boots and the boatman called out, *master, the wind is coming.*

MUTANT

Barbara the tattoo artist sat her dumpy breasts astride my arm and examined my right bicep.

I told her I wanted it plain. I didn't want any fantastical decoration.

A large red strawberry pockmarked with green pips squeezed and stretched across her chest as she sketched out a cheetah's head.

'Small ears', she remarked. 'Not a lion ... not a leopard ... a cougar or a puma?'

'Cheetah', I insisted.

She shivered all the way down to her hips. 'Cheetahs look too female, don't you think?'

I glanced at her gallery of tattoos. There were Chinese and Celtic symbols. There was an American Indian headdress fixed onto Geronimo's head. There were snakes of various colours and there were women ready made for men's muscles.

'I want it exact', I told her.

Barbara looked at me. 'I'm an artist', she said. She smiled. 'You must make room for my imagination'.

She sat up straight and pulled down the neckline of her dress. An iris flower petal fluted out. I stared at its blueness. I imagined its roots lay near her nipple.

The iris twisted as she breathed. The more I looked, the more its blue colour disseminated into individual lines, like veins, looping, gnashing, popping and pooling.

I shook my eyes away.

'And this', Barbara said.

She slipped one foot from her high-class sandal and arched her toes on a small cushioned stool.

The whole of her left sole was covered in multi-coloured fish scales. Bronze, platinum, gold, taupe, purple, orange, green and red scales that scooped and dizzied from the base of her toes to the deep lines at her ankle bone.

She turned her foot to face me. It was blank with ordinary flesh.

'I'm an expert', she promised.

I glanced down at my bicep. It twitched slightly. Barbara brushed her fingers over my skin.

'It's good', she said. 'Tight'. She pursed her lips and turned my arm to its left, then its right. 'I'm seeing how the cheetah will move on you', she said.

She outlined the cheetah from the top of my bicep, across my muscle and its tail flowed into the concave at my elbow. Its haunches stood on the lower rise of my bicep. Its own muscle reached across mine. Its belly, its paws, then its jaw at the rim of my shoulder, and black felt-tip smudges for its markings.

Barbara put down her pen and examined her work so far. She shook her head.

'Cheetah yellow will not be a good colour against your skin', she said. She snapped her fingers trying to think of a description to explain why. 'Your skin is too pasty to begin with … too *bleh*'.

She brushed the back of her hand along the outline of my cheetah. 'His yellow will be lost on you. It won't stand out'.

'I want it exact', I reminded her.

Barbara glanced up at her gallery of tattoo beasts and pointed at a large orange-bristled dragon. It had blue fins and a large Day-Glo green moustache.

'I don't believe in dragons', I said.

Barbara rolled out a laugh. 'Jesus ... no one does'. She patted her chest. 'A tattoo says something about you'.

Cheetah, I thought. Cheetah.

Barbara pointed at a woman wearing a leather bikini and carrying a fur-trimmed spear.

'Maybe you're into that', she suggested.

'I just want the cheetah', I said. 'I want it exactly as it is in the book'.

Barbara concentrated on the animal's back, and as she inlaid the detail for its paws she mentioned, 'maybe this is too big for you?'

She ran her eyes over my torso and other arm. 'Maybe try something neat. Something that would fit on your hip or the back of your wrist'.

'No', I insisted. 'A cheetah is what I want'.

She sat back and admired the black stencil on my bicep.

'You've got good arms for ink', she said. 'Work out much?'

I looked down at her drawing. The cheetah's eyes stared at me.

'You forgot its tear lines', I said.

Barbara bit open her felt-tip pen. 'Sorry', she said. She leaned over my arm. She had a smell of apple and sweat. I watched her draw in the tear lines.

'During the day they can see up to five kilometres', I said.

'*Uh huh*', Barbara said.

'The tear lines help them focus'.

Barbara shifted on her chair and ran her fingers over a standing tray of ink bowls.

'I like your ...', her fingers flashed out in a wide fan, '... your plainness'. She nodded over at her tattoo galleries. 'Sometimes people want weird things, you know?'

I nodded that I knew.

Barbara tapped the middle of her forehead. 'I've got imagination, you know?'

I nodded that I knew that as well.

'My yellow is going to look foul on your skin', she told me.

'I don't mind', I said.

'Well I mind', she said. 'That's my creation on your arm. It has to look so damn good, other people will want it for themselves'.

I looked at her. 'It's a bet', I said.

'Oh God', Barbara said. 'I hate doing bets'. She glanced at her needles. 'You probably don't want the cheetah after all. You're just stuck with some bet with the lads down at the pub'.

She picked up a needle packet and rolled it between her fingers. She smiled at me.

'But bets are my bread and butter'.

She touched my skin.

'I can make him mutant though', she said.

I shifted in my chair. The cheetah's ears seemed to turn.

'A bet, eh?' Barbara encouraged.

I didn't want to tell her but the soft buzz of the tattoo gun, the sensation of smoke rising from my skin, made me confess, 'I'm not a real man'.

She lifted her gun, stared at me for a second, then blew away the small bubbles of blood and extra ink on my bicep.

'Sure you are', she said professionally.

I nodded at the cheetah. 'Too female', I reminded her.

She laughed, shook her head.

'You have great muscles'.

She placed her gun's needle into a shallow bowl of blue ink.

'My favourite colour', she added. She pressed the needle into the cheetah's ears.

'I want shadowing', I said.

Barbara looked up at me.

'You did one of the lads a couple of weeks ago, and he wasn't happy with your shadowing. He said his tattoo didn't move'.

Barbara stopped her work. 'Who was that?'

'Terry'.

Barbara put down her gun, wiped her hands and took out a cigarette packet.

'If you don't smoke, you can sue me'.

I laughed. I liked Barbara. I liked her heavy hips, her tight and rippled waist, the squat strawberry on her torso, the tiny iris hidden beneath her dress and underneath her ordinary foot, her brilliant fish sole with its rasp of scales. I breathed in, almost feeling those scales.

I said, 'I'll have one of those'.

She watched me smoke.

'Terry', she said. 'He tried it on. Squirt of a man. Not in my wildest nightmares'.

I laughed. She stared at me.

'You shouldn't laugh so much. It makes you too nice'.

She blew out her smoke then pulled up the sleeve of her dress to show a large bruise like a splattered green flower on the inside of her lower arm.

'You ever give a woman something like this?'

'No', I said.

'Then you're fine as a man', she said.

She got off her chair, went over to her coffee machine, filled two cups and handed me one.

'Tell me about the bet', she said and sat back in her chair.

'The cheetah', I said.

'He'll wait'. She smiled at me. 'I like stories', she explained.

Terry caught sight of my penis in the pub's urinals.

'Not much there, is there, fella?'

He hit my shoulder. 'Just joking', he said.

I wiped my hands dry with paper towels. 'Ok', I said.

'Ok', he mimicked.

I said nothing then. Terry stared at my face.

'Come on, come on', he whispered. 'Come on, come on'.

I hit him then. My fist crunched on his nose. He went down, clutching and catching blood.

I had to wash my hands again. Terry was still on the floor so I stepped over him on my way out to the bar. The others had bought more drinks.

I sat down.

'Ok?' they said.

'Fine', I said.

They looked over my head. 'Where's Terry?' they said.

'Mopping blood', I said.

They laughed a little bit then went back to their drinks. When Terry joined us, there was only a blush of pink on his nose.

'I'm glad you hit him', Barbara said.

She put down her coffee and resumed tattooing me.

She was working on the cheetah's head. I watched its flesh stand out from my own. The faint blue seeped darker.

Terry had flexed his arm, and the tattoo of a woman just lay there doing nothing.

'Her belly is supposed to move', he complained.

I looked at the woman on his skin.

'Not a great choice', I said.

Terry looked at me. 'What would you know?'

Surrounded by his friends, he was brave.

I sucked up my lager. 'Fifties pin up', I said. 'Cheap and plenty'.

Terry smiled. 'You'd do better, I suppose'.

I nodded.

'What with?' Terry sneered.

I thought for the next few seconds. Then I said, 'a cheetah'.

Terry laughed. 'A fucking cheetah?' He looked at the others, giving them permission to laugh also. I finished my lager.

'A cheetah is a ponce's tattoo', Terry said.

I shrugged. 'I like cheetahs. I like how they run'. I stared at Terry. 'Mine will move so damn good, you'll want it for yourself'.

Barbara smiled when I told her that.

I thought of her fish sole.

And thinking of it I could feel water against my skin.

'You cold?' she asked. 'Goose pimples aren't good for my work'.

She turned and switched her electric heater on.

She smiled at me. Her hair was in her eyes. I brushed it off.

'Thanks', she said.

Her apple sweat was delicious.

Cheetahs would like apples, I thought. I imagined lying in a tree in an African savannah, training my five-kilometre stare on the grass, watching for Thomson's gazelles or wildebeest.

My skin warmed up.

The cheetah moved on my bicep. Its jaw flexed at my shoulder. Its tail switched inside my elbow. Its spots jostled as I tightened and released. Its mutant blue looked like the sky near its belly, then deepened over its haunches and back.

A night sky lay above its ears, plush dark fur on its tear lines and along the rim of its jaw, while its teeth brightened white, whiter than my pasty skin.

'*Grrrrrr*', Barbara growled.

She finished the paws and the tip of the tail.

'Done', she said.

She reached for her cold coffee and another cigarette.

'Show me your foot', I said. 'Please'.

She lifted her foot out of its sandal and I crouched forward to align my cheetah with her fish sole.

'Mutants', I said.

Terry said he was uncomfortable in my presence.

'You've got this female vibe', he said.

The others smiled and looked from me to him.

'It's your hair', Terry said. 'It flops about too much'.

I cut my hair. I razored it to my skull.

'Your muscles aren't so good either', Terry said.

I muscled up. I graded their thickness and practiced in front of a mirror.

And still Terry didn't love me.

I found him in the pub. He was sitting alone.

'I've something to show you', I said.

He nodded and I worked up my shirtsleeve.

My cheetah gleamed in the pub's window light. She nuzzled my shoulder and eased her limbs over my flesh. Her blueness swallowed up my skin.

'Jesus', Terry said.

He reached and touched her.

'I want her', he said after a while.

I said nothing. I ate some crisps and drank some lager.

He followed me out into the street. He followed me to my door.

He said, 'let me sleep with your cheetah'.

I sat him in my kitchen then I opened my knife drawer and handed him a small carving knife.

I said, 'get rid of that cheap bitch on your bicep'.

I watched Terry for as long as it took him to dig her out of his arm while I thought of my cheetah lying in her tree, her eyes on her prey, slowly marking the one she wanted.

A Sense of How Things Feel

I put myself into an Andrew Wyeth painting once. It's his famous *Christina's World*. She wears a pink dress and is lying down on yellow/brown scrub grass. She is crippled from the waist down and in the distance there is a grey farmhouse facing the adjacent horizon. Look at that painting and it is easy to imagine the landscape curl into gulping folds of earth and abyss.

People forget what an animal the imagination is. They would prefer to think the brain is a machine given to odd pictures at times, as if the neurons are bored and wondering what psychological magic they can electrocute the conscious mind with.

So I put myself into an Andrew Wyeth painting. I stepped to one side of Christina and I followed the grass ruts to the house. There was a ladder leaning against the roof gutter. There was a sound of nothing. Just the sky and the horizon like a slinking cat on the ground.

I lit a cigarette. I entered the house. A piece of meat lay on brown paper on the table and flies were high on its blood. The flies dispersed and I looked at the meat. It was round and flat and had a thin wire of fat around its edge. It had a hung odour, ripe, and if I looked too close maybe I'd see maggots ingesting there.

The house was full of that nothing sound. Full and bright and hot and the smell mixed human and animal. The smell of dirty skin and faecal detritus. A cat meowed under the stove. I hunkered down to make it think that I liked it. I presumed it was female and I treated it as such. It looked at my face, at my tie and my neck, and it launched teeth and claws at me, but I back-knifed fast into the middle of the room, then I hit it down with my fist.

The cat limped into a corner.

I looked around for something to drink. There was water in a jug so I had that by the window and I watched Christina drag herself across the grass towards the house. She stopped after a couple of seconds. She crooked her body from her waist up and turned as slow as a tortoise as she surveyed her world.

I knew certain things. I knew she wasn't real. I knew she was made up of two women – herself and Andrew Wyeth's wife. Slightly Frankenstein. The cat curled around my shoes. Good cat, I thought as I watched Christina. She turned her head as if she was staring at the horizon. Something flipped on the washing line outside. A man's trousers, I considered or maybe just a rag of nothing, something brought in over the fields and left on the line to wither.

The water was settling my vomit.

'Ha', I said out loud just to punch the sound of nothing in my head.

Christina's house gobbled up my shout. So I twisted my way into the small corridor of the kitchen. I knew from my research that Christina kept her perishable food in a cellar beneath the hallway floor. I tapped my feet along until I found it. Underneath the small trap door was just earth and I had to imagine small receptacles of milk and squares of butter wrapped in grease paper. Lying there on my stomach I smelled the clay and I felt my blood come right up into my face. The cat rubbed her paws on my back.

'Hmm, hmm', she said as if she were human, which I had no intention of believing.

I stood up, stepped over the cat and walked up the stairs.

It's pale-painted up there and full of that nothing sound.

A man can die in any one of those rooms. He can turn himself off and be nothing.

I settled myself into the room where Andrew Wyeth first saw Christina dragging herself on her hands. He put those hands of hers into the painting but he supplanted Christina's body with his wife's torso and with his wife's head.

His imagination was bringing him into a romantic ideal.

I could understand that. Everyone wants an ideal.

I stared down at Christina's still figure and I imagined her hipbones beneath her dress. I imagined the sound she would make as she pulled herself over the grass. The grunt and shoosh of her breath, the small scrapes along the underside of her arms and the thrust of her jaw as she willed her body forward.

I stood in the room upstairs and felt all that nothing surround me as I focussed on Christina. She had stopped moving. She lay pink and black on the grass. Her legs splayed out and her heels twitched, then stilled.

My father once said that I had too much imagination. He said it was a woman's thing. Something about their minds he couldn't understand. You had to fight against that thing. He knew how to fix a car. He knew tubes of brake fluid. He hit my head once when I said the brake fluid reminded me of a bronze snake.

'Hah', I said out loud again and the room's silence swallowed up my voice.

I turned and walked out of the room, down the short hallway and into another. It was possibly a bedroom. I put a bed there. An iron bed with springs, something that would make noise. I put photographs that I had taken with my Dad's old camera on the wall.

One of my non-existent and ex-girlfriends had asked me once, 'how come you don't live in the modern world?'

She meant all things digital and snappy.

She clicked her fingers at me. 'Instant', she said. She took a photograph of the pair of us. I had been bald then. She said the lack of hair showed up my features but after a while she complained that I wasn't good in bed and she also complained that I didn't act like a hunter anymore.

That was the first thing she liked about me, she said. My far-off stare that zeroed into her. I told her I was a writer and she said that possibly accounted for the stare.

She said, 'what kind of things do you write?'

I positioned a saltcellar between us, then I added a tiny bowl of butter. We were having breakfast and I was already bored. The thing about hunting and the imagination is that after a while things begin to stink. The prey stinks and your imagination can't pretty that up.

I handed her a pile of my stories.

She sat at the table and read for half an hour. She had a method I hated. A quick glance over the first few sentences then a scan down over the end lines on the page before moving onto the next.

After while she said, 'I don't think I like your writing. Nothing happens'.

I stared over at her face. She had this French style to her make-up and her clothes. Sometimes she was ugly and fascinating, other times she was bland and pink and smelled too clean and full of soap.

That day she was clean but I wanted her ugly.

I rang one of my sisters and asked, 'how do you make someone love you?'

'I don't know', my sister said. 'I absolutely don't'.

I began to grow my hair and my girlfriend got bored. She said she found someone else. I said ok. She stared at me and said my trouble was that my empathy was barely skin deep.

I rang my brother and asked him to describe empathy to me. He laughed and said just be thankful the bitch left you. He said maybe now you can get a real job. I heard one of his kids in the background. They sounded normal. I laughed and said I had a job. I put words on paper. My brother laughed back. We sounded fine as we laughed. We sounded brotherly.

In that upstairs bedroom of Christina's house my photographs looked good on the wall. They were mainly of my family. Mum, Dad, sisters and brother. There were photographs of our house in Sydney and the trees and swing in the back garden.

It was easy to stand in that garden now and look back through the living room window and watch how the adults lived their lives, how they touched or didn't touch. My parents glided by each other, hips steering sideways, eyes not looking.

That's when I began to put things in where they never existed. That's how I began to feel things without touching them.

I put a mattress on the bed, then a sheet, then a blanket.

The cat padded in. I closed my eyes and I lay down.

I thought of Christina dragging her body over the dirt ground that led to the house. I saw the low sun on the grass and that wind turn as usual and whip the rag on the line.

Imagination had been my mother's defence at the slight sociopathic tendencies of my father. She collected books of paintings and she painted also. She stared at a blank canvas as if she was hunting something inside it. I wanted to be like her but I could feel my father inside me as well. That way of looking at things as a snake looks at its prey.

Don't hit her, I had pleaded with Dad once and he had stared at me as if I was nothing. Mum was on the bed, curled up and the room was almost dark because of the curtains.

Don't hit her, I said again.

It sounded good to say things like that. It sounded caring.

'Your father doesn't know how to love', Mum told us.

My sister got pregnant very quickly. She said she could love this way, couldn't she? I just nodded by her hospital bed. It was winter in Sydney. The wind was blowing. My sister had met this guy and was moving to Paramatta with the new baby. My brother was pissed off since the guy was some Lebanese Christian and as far as he was concerned, that sort were two steps from a god-forsaken life in a medieval desert.

I laughed. 'Parramatta is a desert'.

My brother said, 'I'm going to do it different'.

He married a blonde girl from Sydney University who used to moonlight in a music shop. They bonded over vintage *Midnight Oil*. She was nice. They had three kids. My brother got middle-aged before his time and I saw our father creeping into him. The blonde wife was skittish and laughed a lot. I recognised that laugh. I hated it everytime I heard it. My brother hated it as well. He slapped her once to make it stop. His kids drooled orange juice in shock. When I was leaving, my sister-in-law said, 'he doesn't do it often'.

In Paramatta my sister began to drink a little in the mornings. Not too much but enough to give the day a clearer light, she said. Her husband was fine, couldn't ask for better really, but he didn't understand her insides.

'Remember my insides, Leon?'

I didn't know anything about her insides but I nodded because she was slightly drunk and her kid looked weird staring at me.

'What's with the bald head?' my sister said.

I told her that I had shaved off my hair to look less like Dad.

He laughed when I visited him with his new family. He dug his fingers into the base of my skull and said, look at this son of mine, Caroline.

His Caroline came over and tapped her knuckles on my skull.

'That's where you get all your stories, eh?'

She didn't believe what Dad had been like. She said he was good to her and to her two kids. I watched him that day, acting the husband and father. I asked if it was as easy as it looked. He said, 'you need a drink after asking a question like that'.

'I need a bloody answer, Dad'.

'You're just like your mother', Dad said. 'You're never letting me go'.

I stared at him. He was older. His skin had thickened and turned grey.

You have to have a sense of how things feel, Mum used to say whenever she looked at something before she painted it. Breadcrumbs on the breakfast counter – zero in your eyes and imagine each facet of a crumb as you would image the major facets of an atom. The crevices, the tiny holes, and the abysses. Become so small that you can step in and explore.

Dad turned his head to me. 'Stop staring'.

My first girlfriend also said, 'stop staring'.

We were in MacDonalds in Sydney's Central Plaza, chewing on burgers and I was fast-guzzling a chocolate milkshake. I was fat and determined to make an effort at sex. My first girlfriend ate like a bird. I focussed on her clavicle. It stood out from her neck and I wanted to touch her there. I thought of the words to describe it. Almost triangular, deep but narrow bridged, freckles or a collection of moles on the left bone – her right – and the skin was suntanned mocha. It would feel crease free. Nothing like the chests of older women, crackled in their thirties with small fissures that catered to sweat trickles.

My girlfriend burped. I could hear it in Christina's room.

The cat stretched along the windowsill.

We did it in my bedroom when the house was empty. We didn't talk. Her hair got into my mouth. Her clavicle smelled of lemons. Her breath smelled of MacDonald's burger. My legs fitted inside hers. Our eyes slid nowhere near each other's. There was just this small noise and my bed bumped against the wall.

I tried to feel. I tried to get deep. I tried to feel love and afterwards I watched her pull her hair back and clip it into a high and messy tail.

'That was good', I said.

'Yeah, it was ok', she said.

She stared at herself in the mirror. 'I look like shit'.

'I love you', I told her.

She laughed at me. 'Ok'.

I was sixteen. I thought that was what you were supposed to tell them.

The first time I saw *Christina's World* was in my mother's painting room, which was also the utility room at the back of the house. She had found the print in some op-shop in West Ryde. She propped it up on the top-loader washer and stood back to admire the light on the picture. I stared at Christina's body. I saw the veins in her hands and the lines of her back. I could feel her nails dig into the first layer of the hard earth. I looked at what she was looking –

the tall house on the horizon, and I felt something open inside me as I stood there beside my mother. I remember that it was almost forty degrees in the shade and water was restricted and my mother was breathing heavily and her skin had blistered pink as it always did in the summer.

She smiled and ruffled my hair. I saw a bruise just beneath her chin.

I began to write after that.

My father said get a real job, so I got one in his garage. I inked up with oil during the day and at night I wrote stories that made no sense and even later at night I stared at Christina lying in her field. I stared so hard I could imagine the tiny leaves of grass twist then flatten underneath her body.

The cat meowed.

I listened to it with my eyes closed. Not yet, I told it. Not yet but it meowed louder and longer until it screeched, until I had to accept that it was the intercom buzzer and Christina's room dissolved around me until there was nothing left but my own room with its large desk, its bed and its added-on kitchenette.

I stood up from the carpet and readied myself.

My first client of the afternoon was a man. He wondered if he could smoke. I handed him an ashtray, then I sat behind my desk, clicked on a pen and moved some papers. He smiled and blew out his smoke. His hair was butter-brown and it curled in ice cream waves above the thin cone of his face. He said he was amazed someone like me even existed.

I said that I was fulfilling a forgotten niche.

The man stared at the Christina print on the wall behind my head.

'Jesus, she's everywhere, isn't she?'

After Mum died, I had tried to put her back together again. I tried to figure up her bones through words, then her flesh, then her eyes, then odd pictures of her with salt and vinegar drenched chips in her mouth. Sometimes I wrote her into the sidelines of school footy matches. Other times I'd put her beside Dad, laughing but with no sound coming out.

After her death Dad burned *Christina's World* so I grew my hair long and dark to my collar. The kids in school said, *what are you – boy or girl* and my penis shrank for a while.

From grief, some doctor surmised.

One girlfriend tried to uncurl it back to its original length. She laughed. I laughed. At a funeral I told a mourning woman that I could make her lover come back to life in a metaphorical manner. She offered me a drink. She said she felt sorry for me. I was a good-looking kid. I wrote her a story about her dead husband from her own words. She put it inside her bra next to her heart. She kissed me. Her lips were dry with scaly corners.

You have to have a sense of how things feel.

I travelled to Europe. Grief was good business in Europe and it was better in Ireland. People wanted to do something new with their grief. They went away with the pages I had written for them and they said they slept better. Once or twice I mentioned that I was really a writer but they didn't believe me.

I got old in Ireland. One day I woke up with a large pain in my head and my room was quiet. I looked at Christina. I was nearly thirty-nine and I was nothing.

I picked up my pen.

'What's the name of the deceased?'

'No one', the man said. He laughed and produced his card and it stated in first letter curling capitals: *De-Bunker of Liars, Con Men and Un-Desirable Aliens From Other Countries.*

'I'm a grief counsellor', I said.

'You are a failed writer, mate. A cut-price Frankenstein. Making up futures for dead people'.

The man's accent was Australian. His tongue flicked forward and his ice cream hair slipped further back from his ears. He tapped his fingers on my paper.

'No empathy. No substance. No voice. Isn't that what publishers tell you?'

He took my pen and drew an open mouth with no tongue.

I saw lips and teeth and the shading made the tonsils stand out.

No tongue. No voice. I laughed and glanced about my room.

'Are you real?' I said without looking at the man.

He did not reply.

I twisted to look at Christina and the photographs beside her.

'Is he real?' I said to them.

I turned back but the man had disappeared and the room was cold.

I got up from my desk, entered my kitchenette, found more pills and poured water into a glass. I imagined them racing to obliterate the pain.

I stared into *Christina's World*. I took an extra pill.

Outside my window there were the usual noises of life and I thought of my old life in Sydney and how faraway it was and I kept staring at Christina on the wall, and I took another pill and I wondered how long more it would take to walk up the grass rutted road again, step inside the front door of Christina's house and up to that quiet, soundless room and lie down and wait for something to keep me alive.

THE MERCENARY'S STORY

He sat down to ostrich steak with the rest of them and drank his beer. He said he was celebrating. His wife was pregnant and it would be his seventh child.

He was in a funny mood and the other men were careful to keep him smiling. They were all good friends. They were old men with families in their backgrounds although the mercenary was slightly younger, still slightly wilder, and the sort of man you would not dispute with unless you knew his temper was good for the night.

The mercenary mopped up his gravy, then stared at the bottle of unopened Champagne in the middle of the table.

'Who drinks that piss?'

The mercenary's name was Rolf Kotze. His mother was living her last days in a nursing home back in Jo'burg. He rarely visited her. He was afraid of her eyes. He could not explain this to anyone. Not least to any of the black nurses that usually attended her. He had to swallow spit in order to address them and he knew that they could see him. They could see his thick ankles in his *vellies*. His khaki boy shorts and his white blond hair.

The nurses were polite. They said his mother was still beautiful.

Rolf knew that they were lying. His mother was thin and old and always situated under the window. Her small white head looked at him from there. Her eyes had remained large. Staring at her he could no longer remember her young or even real.

Rolf gestured at the Champagne. 'Whose piss?'

'Mine', one of his friends said.

This friend was Irish. He was one of those men who had left his family some years ago and had decided that Africa was now his home. An ageing man who had only ever had small soft terrors in his life, but he was getting older and the loneliness was making him drink.

Rolf liked the Irishman. One of his great-grandmothers had been Irish.

'What are we celebrating?' Rolf asked.

The Irishman leaned over on his elbows. His words came out slow.

'I got married'.

The other old men looked at their plates and their knives.

'Married?' Rolf said.

He thought who would take an old Irishman who bakes his own bread?

'Her name is Joanne'.

'Good name', Rolf said.

He sliced out a piece of his steak and put it in his mouth. This marriage was not right. He could smell its stink. He swallowed. He waited for something more to be said.

'We married in the Lutheran church'.

'*Hmm, hmmm*', Rolf said, waiting for more.

'But before that ...'

'Yes?'

'I put a knife into the neck of her father's favourite cow'.

There was the stink. Rolf felt his nostrils burn like fire.

'She is *kaffir*, then, eh?'

The Irishman ignored him and began to unwire the Champagne bottle top.

Rolf thought, another one, another one of those bleeding old men's hearts with livers to match.

'Piss', Rolf said.

He hated the clear liquid in his new glass. It sparkled too much. It would give him wind, and somewhere in his gut a hate stirred. A thick, lush hate and it twined around his bowel to give him the satisfaction of a fart.

It smelled of iron and warm ostrich.

'Is your *piel* really that small, eh?' Rolf asked the Irishman.

'Shut up, Rolf', someone said.

Rolf laughed. 'You think that is a good story, my friends?'

The men shifted in their chairs. It was almost two o'clock in the next morning. They wanted to sleep and the Irishman had a new wife who was turning down his pillows.

'I can tell you a good story', the mercenary said.

He swallowed some beer then began.

'Some years ago before all this life eh … I was out walking with my gun in my parents' veld. I was young and it was over to my right that I spied a black abusing a dog. So I lifted my rifle and I got him right between the eyes'.

The mercenary took another drink from his beer. He saw his gun as if it was still in his hands. He could feel the hard steel, almost taste it in his mouth. The dog disappeared into the bush. The black man lay on the ground with a hole in his forehead. The blood was red, quite red.

Rolf rubbed his right hand on his shorts then he smiled and raised a glass of the Champagne.

'I can tell you other stories', he promised. 'Good stories'.

They tried not to listen but he told them.

After he had killed the black, he said, he had gone home and his mother's eyes were strange as if she could smell the black's blood. He wanted to tell her that he had just killed something but he did not like her eyes.

His mother sat in a chair on the veranda. She stared at the veld. His father came out of the house smelling of toothpaste and beer. He looked at the boy's gun and grunted. The boy put down his gun and put his hands on his mother's knees. He tried to look into her eyes but they had swum away from him and suddenly he was glad he had killed something that morning.

Something real.

The dead black was real. The dog was real.

Something had to be real.

PERSEPHONE

After they die, they change. It is not visible at first. Their skin does not wither. It does not fall, nor does it drip, and so the dead pat their faces, eager to believe that their eyes will remain exact, that their fingers, old or young, will still grasp and touch. They look at me, relieved that I look as whole as I was the day I was taken here. They glance at Hades and I smile as if to assure them that even love survives in hell.

Eurydice runs after me, amazed at the life in her still. Is it true, she demands, is it true that I am always as I am now? I tell her yes. Her face is grey but beautiful. I feel spit in the back of my throat. I hold it there, not wanting to strike her as the viper had struck her, yet part of me looks forward to the moment when her skin will begin to change, but by then she will not know and she will not care.

Their noses first, flattening wide like swine nostrils, then their eyes deepening black into the last shreds of their skulls. Their reason diminishes until they crawl like bloodless infants and I step over them, letting my robes move in and out of their shaded forms.

But Tiresias – Tiresias, I have kept sane.

I watch him as he mumbles among the dead, and his mind works all the edges of his brain. Eurydice chatters alongside him. She chatters of her Orpheus and the old seer bows his head, and I can see the inner workings of his ear, the pale trail of blood that still feeds his blind eyes, and if I look further down his body I see the outline of his heart. It does not pump.

Tiresias's faint nose sniffs Eurydice's hair. His mouth opens and what used to be his tongue falls through his lips. Eurydice sniffs also. Her wide, almost blank eyes swim towards me.

'The pomegranate, wasn't it?' she wonders, then casts her head to one side, smiling at Hades who sits on his throne.

Perhaps Orpheus had adored that gesture, and Hades likes pretty things. He likes nymphs. The last one, Minthe, I turned into a plant.

'I persuaded her to eat a few seeds of pomegranate', Hades answers Eurydice.

This is the way Hades likes to tell his story. He tells it from one true point, then he adds the lie. I did eat but not from him.

My husband likes to imagine that he feeds me. He likes to believe that he has kept me here at his own will. He told that same story to Peirithous who had once tried to carry me back to Earth as his bride.

Peirithous said he loved me.

Love. I had forgotten how it could be.

Hades was cordial, gentlemanly and sweet.

He insisted that only the most recent dead serve our guest. Peirithous ate or drank, yet he sat in the chair that Hades offered him, and as Peirithous settled his flanks, Hades smiled with all the diplomacy and malignancy he has in common with Zeus, my father, his brother.

Hades poured the wine. The wine smelt sweet and rich. I drank the wine. It faded to nothing beyond my teeth.

Then I watched as the chairs turned into serpents. Peirithous screamed. A man's body can switch like a snake's if the venom is powerful enough. The grey scales smoothed out the dark beautiful brown of Peirithous's skin and leavened it into the arms of the chair, the chair of Forgetfulness, and the chair of Lethe. It consumes humans.

'I loved her so much I wanted her forever', Hades tells Eurydice who sighs and dreams of Orpheus, while her face, although not changed too much yet, shifts and moves with her lover's memory.

'She still has pretty feet', I say aloud to no one. Her heels are shining bright like fresh oysters. I feel my spit stir.

Eurydice stops smiling. 'Still?' she murmurs, wary of the word. 'Still?'

She glances back at Tiresias. 'Still?' she asks him.

His brain stirs inside his skull.

'Queen', he warns. 'Queen, do not play with the dead'.

'He gave me nothing', I tell Eurydice. 'I took seven seeds from the pomegranate. The gardener told Hades'.

Hades smiles. He twists his nails into his palms. I remember how he twisted his hand into me that first and last day. I remember that as I picked the narcissus flower, the huge wheel of Hades chariot grazed my face and the earth peeled back and the dead looked up.

'*I* kept myself here', I persist at him. '*I*'.

Tiresias's blind eyes stare into me.

More than anything of the dead, he understands how I have remade myself. Even as the remnants of the seeds lay between my teeth, old Tiresias sat me down and laid out my power for me, while my mother cried in a far corner and my father rumbled from above, and Hades persisted that what he had done was done from love.

I saw my power. I saw it as if it was a layer of the finest silk and it stretched the length of Hades's table.

'Imagine it further', Tiresias whispered inside my ear. His speech was still hot with life. 'Imagine it across everything you see and touch'.

I imagined it across Hades. I imagined it smothering him and although I knew that was not possible now, the thought of it made me smile, and at that moment the girl I was finally died and I was born instead.

Persephone. The Goddess of Death.

Eurydice flitters before me. She is crying now, running her fingers through her breasts. Hades embraces me. I feel the string of his muscles beneath his robe. It is not love. It is only what Tiresias advised me to imagine. It is a survival. Sometimes it is comforting because I have grown used to it.

His breath is clay-scented. His lips are cold. He leaves me with Eurydice who is still crying for Orpheus. Her calls for him crack against the walls of the Underworld but soon, very soon, she is like the others, hitching her shadow to their shadow forms, melting into them, and her eyes dart back and forth and into other skulls, lost now, then found. Lost again and frantic through the dead air, sometimes buzzing against my face and one day Orpheus comes.

Hades and I sit on our thrones and we listen to him play his lyre and sing for his wife. I do not want to listen. I do not want to see my husband melt for one human and not for me. I could have sung like that and had my freedom. Instead I watch my power run after Eurydice as her shadow follows Orpheus.

'Do not look back', Hades had warned him. 'Do not look back until she is in the sun-light'.

My power, my silk reaches into the pretty heels of Eurydice. I feel her shock at being rooted. My mouth opens her mouth. I cry out. Orpheus turns. The sunlight flashes on his face. Eurydice screams or I scream. I see love turn to horror in Orpheus' eyes as he realises that the half-formed thing before him, that collection of blood and floating bones, are the last living things he will ever see of his wife. I thrust my face at his. The sun cracks my skin.

'Gods!' Orpheus cries. 'Gods!'

Above my face the sky turns bright.

Hades plucks me back.

I can still taste the winter sunlight on my lips. I had seen trees without leaves and the ground bare and hard, but living roots and seeds bloated with sap beneath the frost, and the air, oh the air, breathing that air. It pulsed my lungs.

I thought of my mother allowing the ground to die in memory of me and when I had Eurydice's sudden living eyes, I saw what love was. Not a man's love, not even a god's love but my mother's love, bitter and blighted, roaming unwashed into other families, putrefying crops, creating famine and death.

And when I had eaten that fruit, when I saw that the gardener had seen me suck the pomegranate juice and bite the seeds, my hunger went further into me, so far further that I could not feel it, and when my mother Demeter came for me, smelling of filth and rotting vegetables, I felt the pomegranate seeds grit against my teeth.

And Hades said what Hades said.

'She took the seeds from my hand'.

My mother cursed him. She cursed me as well. Could I not have waited? Could I not have trusted her? Could I not see what I had done to her, to myself?

I did not want to tell her that she smelled of real death. I did not want to tell her that with Hades death hardly smelled and that earlier that morning as I had transformed the gardener into a screeching owl, something cold but alive entered me, and I saw my life with Hades. I saw the moments when I would take his love for me and roll it between my fingers until it was as small as a seed for eating.

THE NEW WIFE

The new flat was clean and bright and the new wife seemed happy. It was a day of visiting. First her husband's grandson's father, then his actual daughter. The new wife stared at the small rectangular table in the kitchen. Everything was small. It was compact. Shelves fitted into cupboards and the fridge was rammed tight into its long slot. The new wife lit a cigarette and wondered how she had got this marriage wrong.

The new wife hated being new. The thought of the visitors watching her movements in the bright and open kitchen disturbed her. The coffee canister was hard to open. It was so new that it broke her favourite coloured nail. The shellac snapped off and she was left with just a pink and brown mess, and some blood.

She turned on the radio. She didn't like the accents but her husband liked the news. He was sitting there near the glass doors that opened onto a cement balcony. It was compact as well. When she first saw it she wondered how to hang out a washing line. She was told that the management company wouldn't allow that. They didn't like clothes to be seen. There was a washer and dryer. It was a brilliant invention. Her husband got down on his knees to experiment with the invention. He realised that once the clothes had been washed, they had to be divided into small kilogramme weights to be dried.

His wife straightened her mouth. What kind of stupid invention made you work more?

The radio turned into music. Irish music. It ran up and down inside the wife's ears so she busied herself arranging biscuits on a plate. The grandson's father was easy to talk to and he liked to listen to his own opinions. He and the woman's husband sat and discussed the government and the new flat. He told them about the rubbish collection. He said the management company were good. They were official and they knew how to make the place below serviceable and tidy.

Her husband said he was glad to be here and she knew that was a lie, but they both said it all the time and after a while it meant the truth.

The grandson came the first day of visiting. He was tall for his age and polite, blonde and big in a sturdy, athletic manner. He loved his grandfather. Sometimes that love made the new wife swallow her coffee too fast. Sometimes she wanted the grandson out of her sight so that she could drink a beer and sit in front of the computer and Skype someone that loved her.

Love, she thought. She washed the blood from her finger, then used a plaster to cover up the wound. She played with the shellac and nail remains while she sipped some vodka-spiced water. She glanced at the fridge. She hated the fridge. It was narrow and white looking. The freezer compartment was small. It iced up fast.

Sometimes she saw them looking at her, then looking away. She had got used to that. She had told herself that people were always people. Her husband would always be her husband. He was still sitting there, listening to Irish music. She said to him, 'would you like to listen to news?'

He shook his head.

When the first visitor arrived, the new wife was able to show how content she and her husband were. Her biscuits sat on the plate and looked good. The coffee was too strong in the beginning but she watered it down and the grandson's father was happy. He talked politics.

The new wife felt bored. Politics meant nothing to her. It was mainly men in power and men in power thought they could do anything they wanted. Politics could be in bed beside you or outside in the street waiting for you to appear.

In this country the politics fitted into the television.

The new wife asked, 'when is your daughter arriving?'

Her husband shrugged. His illness sometimes made him slow to answer.

The first visitor laughed, then went on talking. The new wife went to the toilet and re-arranged her hairband. Then she stared at her face.

She was afraid. She was afraid of this world. She was afraid of the flat and its new carpet and she was afraid of the second bedroom where she knew she would sleep because that was all there was to her marriage.

She closed her eyes. She thought – I have a good mind. I have a good soul. My heart is good also.

She had seen a way out. She had taken it.

She went back into the sitting room. Her husband was laughing so she smiled and sat down and ate a biscuit and drank some coffee. The television was on in the background and one of those football games was playing. The commentator's voice was a woman. That had always surprised the new wife. How women in this country talked about sport as if they understood it.

The intercom buzzed. It was her husband's daughter who had brought flowers and cake, who was friendly, who took off her coat and kissed her father and who greeted her nephew's father, then sat down and listened for just a few seconds before putting herself into the politics conversation. The daughter was educated to a point and she tried to understand many things. She was studying history.

She saw the new wife's plastered finger. She said shellac nails were something that she never had the guts to experience. Her nails were short and did the job. She had a good face. It was neat and pretty and pale but it had freckles. Freckles made the new wife laugh. They shocked her funny bone – all those bursts of brown on white skin.

The first visitor was leaving to make dinner for his son. He stood in the middle of the flat and said, 'you'll be happy here'. Everyone agreed with him. The new flat was clean and newly-painted and fitted with everything they could use in a modern home.

The new wife thought of Skyping her sister.

She wanted to say things to somebody who would understand her. The daughter was nearly her age but she would never be a sister.

The daughter sat forward in her seat. 'How many tablets do you have to take?'

'Four', her father answered.

'I have put them in order', the new wife said.

She stared at the daughter and saw how one day that she would probably look like the old wife.

'He will live for years', the new wife said.

She glanced at the biscuits on the plate. She wanted to eat them all and feel full and safe. She went back into the bathroom and sat on the toilet. This new country was having a hot summer but she was afraid of its winter. She had seen pictures before she came here. She had seen videos and spoken to others who had moved into this country and said it was no different from any other country in Europe. It was mostly white but it was liveable.

Someone knocked on the bathroom door. It was the daughter. She said she was going now. The new wife walked to the door with her, then stepped outside into the small hallway.

She said, 'it is so small here but they have made the windows so big'.

The windows let in so much light that whenever the new wife stood in front of them she felt as if she was flying.

The daughter was nearly crying and would not say why. She smiled, kissed the new wife's cheek, wished her happiness, then stepped into the lift and disappeared. The new wife was left alone in the hallway. In the flat opposite was a couple who liked riding bikes and were usually noisy in the mornings as they went to work.

Sometimes the new wife leaned out over the balcony to watch them cycle away. Her husband had said don't fall and she replied that she wouldn't or at least not yet.

The new wife cleaned the table of biscuits and coffee then sat in front of the computer. Her husband sat in front of the television. When she had first known him he had been laughing and easy to drink with. He had never seemed old. Her sister said well, you feel something for him, don't you and she said yes.

Love, she thought. But it didn't fit now. She thought about the daughter. She stared at the computer screen and watched it buzz for a Skype link.

She said out loud, 'why was she crying?'

The old man turned his head. 'I told her where I wanted my body put when I'm dead'.

The new wife nodded. He had told her that long ago. He had told her first. The Skype link lit up and she smiled.

The old man had told her first.

THE SPIDER

It was his version of a house. It had blue curtains on the window and a red kettle on the nearby range. The clock ticked down from the wall. The fire licked up bright and hot. The armchair was hairy to the touch. Even the cat looked feral, its red tongue and its long nails, its orange-furred paws, and its long whine while I searched for milk for it to drink.

You can't let the animal starve, he told me.

I stood my bare feet on the cold slab kitchen floor, watching the night outside the window. He was out there swinging a lamp at moths. Come here, come here to your death, he called out to them. I laughed then I drank some milk. The cat twisted around my ankle. I wanted to kick it but I couldn't. I liked animals because he liked animals. He liked them smelling of kill and death, while I liked them because you are supposed to value pets. You are supposed to love things that are vulnerable.

My husband glanced in at the window and at me. He hadn't asked for dinner but the thought was there. You're the woman with the woman hands. You can magic up real food with seasoning and juice.

I roasted chicken with garlic.

He sat and ate it. Juice dripped from his mouth. I looked at his hands. They were so big with white tipped nails. They were like his words. Big and pouncing.

He said, 'remember that spider we killed?'

He held up the fingers of one hand. 'This big with legs'.

I laughed. He laughed. His smile was gorgeous, I wanted to love him more but I could feel the wall there. Hard and flat like his chest. He once told me that he didn't really know love. All those poems he wrote, they sounded better in animal voices and thoughts. He licked garlic from his knife. I licked it from my fork. We laughed through desert and later the wine felt good. His fingers were in my hair and on my scalp.

The children cried but I ignored them. The cat upset a lamp then yowled and skittered behind the kitchen door. I thought of the spider and how we had killed it.

It had been in this house first. Its webs were in every room. We shucked them down. The dust crawled up and stuck in our nostrils. The children screamed with nightmares. I could not write. He said not to worry. He gave me prompts. Words and situations, magic incantations. He said look at the snot on your son's face. Make it a snail's exodus.

'It's snot', I said. 'There is no snail'.

He said imagine that the snail opened its shell. Imagine your fingers inside.

I imagined something else. I imagined the soft salt crystals of my son's snot. I imagined how it would taste. I imagined the hiccupping sobs in his lungs, how they ran up and down his bronchial tubes like notes in a tune.

My son was crying about the spider.

He said it sat on his bed and would not move. Even when he was sleeping he could feel it walk over his face.

My husband devised a plan for murder.

I told him to do it quick. No thinking. Just a rolled up newspaper and whack it hard.

I was writing when the spider joined me at my desk. At first I saw nothing but a black fuzz out of the corner of my eye. I assumed it was my shortsightedness. For seconds I half-stared at the black mass sitting on my old-fashioned wooden pencil case. I could hear my husband in the garden outside. He had mentioned discovering blackberries. He said we would live off the fat of the land.

I thought of the fat.

Yellow rind or thick grey in the autumn, marbled with blood like blackberry juice. I looked through the window above my writing table. My husband was out there in his wellingtons and his new Aran pullover. His thick hands were full of blackberry branches. The children were screaming and dancing. The air looked cold and vicious, full of stark sunlight and morning mist.

I had met my husband at university. He reminded me of my dead father.

His poems were loud, jumping, black and pouncing.

I admired the way his arms fit into his shirtsleeves, rolled up, then tightened above his elbows and all he needed was the insignia.

The telephone rang. A woman's voice at the other end. I tore it from the wall.

He came in. Big with blackberry bushes. The children were strung to his heels. Their smiles were blackberry dark. I pointed at the spider.

'Kill it', I said.

My husband turned arms first and saw the telephone lying on the ground. I pointed at the motionless spider.

'Kill it', I said.

He killed it fast. One crush and the spider was dead.

'No more nightmares', my husband called to our son.

I placed the spider on my desk. Its eight legs were broken. Its thorax and head were smashed and brittle. My husband moved about in the kitchen, cleaning dishes he rarely ever touched and relaying jokes and giggles with the children. His voice was hollow and huge. It stuck to the ceiling.

I stared down at the spider.

I imagined the other woman's voice. Ripe with vowels and smart with pronounced consonants. A shadow thin woman waiting in the background. Not like me, still thick and lumpy from pregnancy and crippled with milk and children's snot. I imagined the woman's flat stomach and her formed thighs and I imagined the smell of her dark Egypt hair wrapping round and round, and through my husband's fingers.

MAY'S END

May used to accompany her father to cattle markets. She knew how to sell an animal and she knew how to drink in a pub. She could also swear and hawk phlegm like any man. Yet at night, she did ordinary female things such as sew buttons, bake soda bread and wash down the flagstone floor. In her secret times, she'd read one of the books that Elisabeth, the local Protestant school mistress had lent her, and later, after her father had died, she and Jim lived side by side which was the usual way of things in early twentieth century Ireland.

Until Jim fell in love with what he called the local beauty. May felt something cold reach into her heart. The beauty was the local pub landlord's daughter. She had thick black hair and long legs. She wore a thin strip of gauzed-lace white beneath the open collar of her blouse. May could see Jim's eyes crawl to the skin above the gauze. He said he was in love with her. He said he was marrying her. He said he was going to bring her home and they would all live together as a family.

'And then there'll be children', he promised.

Jim's new wife patrolled the length and width of the small room. Her shoes' heels clicked on the flagstone floor. Her nose tipped the lip of the milk jug.

'Sour', she announced.

Jim's wife moved in and May was afraid of her. She was afraid of the changes the new woman brought. May was also afraid of the woman's body and whenever Jim would graze himself against it, May pretended not to look.

She also pretended not to hear the noises from the bedroom, yet she watched as Jim's wife took control of the range, insisting that Jim prefer her bread to May's. Later she demanded that May share the proceeds from the chicken eggs. May refused. Jim took May out to the edge of the lake where they used to wander as children and he tried to talk to her. He tried to tell her that there were things that went on between men and women that she could not understand.

He twisted his fingers one over the other, a little alarmed at his sister's red cheeks, her blue eyes, so blue whenever they looked on him he could see their dead father there.

'It's settled this way', he decided.

One night May sat outside with the dog and drank some porter. She stared up at the sky while the dog snuffled at her feet while inside Jim's wife screamed giving birth. May wished her all the known pain on the earth and later, as she stared at the baby in its crib, she refused to touch it.

Over the days Jim encouraged his sister to love the baby.

'No', his wife said. 'She drinks too much'.

The baby's cries seeped through the house and so did Jim's happiness. His wife tightened her dresses about her and moulded her figure back into its original shape. She made the soda bread and put the chicken money into a new post office account. She paraded her and Jim's child. A fat baby sleeping in a carriage ordered from Dublin.

Lambswool blankets and fine cotton bonnets.

May began to notice the different smiles people gave her. They pitied her living in a house with another woman. It meant the power had changed. It meant that she was something extra. Something to be brushed aside once the housework was completed.

May brought a book back to Elisabeth the school mistress and asked, 'is it wrong to hate so much?'

Elizabeth wore a green pleated wool skirt and a light pink blouse. She wore glasses also, but she took them off, all the better to see May standing there, fingering the edges of the cloth draped over the table at the window.

May stared out at the garden. It was so green she felt she could disappear down into it and sleep. 'I only want it and her gone'.

She rubbed granuels of dirt over the surface of the table cloth. The dirt came from a plant pot of peonies placed on the table. Next to it was a small tower of books. May read names and titles – *Ethan From* by Edith Warton, *In a German Pension* by Katherine Mansfield. There was Tennyson, whom she had already read. There was H.G Wells and Yeats.

'What does it look like?' Elisabeth asked.

May did not want to say what it looked like.

'I shiver when I approach a baby', Elisabeth said. 'They look so fragile and foreign'.

'Things will change, May', Elisabeth promised.

Things changed on a late Autumn morning when Jim went out into his field and looked at the horizon. He was in his early thirties and still young. He loved his wife but he was growing wary of his sister. He was glad that there were rules to follow. He knew that a wife takes precedence over a sister. He had watched his wife aim the narrow heel of her shoes onto the kitchen floor. This is mine, he had almost heard her say.

'This is mine', he thought and then his heart cracked. It cracked from his chest to his arm. The world froze. The field, the trees, the sky stopped and Jim fell dead onto his field.

Jim's wife and sister hated each other's grief. It was as if Jim's ghost had materialised between them and Jim's wife would not let May touch the baby, and after the funeral, May returned home to find all her belongings in the yard outside.

Jim's baby cried while Jim's wife sat at the kitchen table and watched May, who then gathered up her belongings and went to live with the Protestant school mistress who in her turn showed May to a room, then showed her to her brother, Gerard.

Here she is. All for you.

Elisabeth's brother Gerard had loved May for years. Finally he had her and he married her and May wanted for nothing for the rest of her life.

Elisabeth said, 'you see, there are happy endings sometimes'.

But May's didn't know what love was supposed to be. The damp feel of a man's body was so real in contrast to any story in a book, and sometimes when she went out to the horses to listen to their breath and rub their hides, so unlike the hides of cattle, she remembered the pubs she and her father spent market day evenings in – the sound of spit and talk. The men with sweat on their faces, the feel of money in her palm and the fierce brilliant feeling of still being herself.

HOW I MURDERED LUCREZIA

She had this pristine thing going on, like she was porcelain, you know, and I wanted to be her friend, but she just didn't like anything about me, so me and the boy who once got together with her – and I mean really together – well, we talked and I said it wasn't fair that some people thought they were better than us, and he said he thought the same. Then I said, my Dad's got a gun somewhere and we could shoot her if you like, and he laughed, you know the way you laugh when you're not supposed to really want something but deep down that's all you want? So I waited until my parents were out somewhere and I went to the shoe box in the back of my mom's wardrobe and I took the gun and I put the bullets in and then I took it to the boy, and I said to him, 'you've got to do it because she broke your heart and that means more than her breaking mine'.

I thought it was romantic. So we waited until the girl was in the playground just after recess and everybody was on the way back to class and he called her name. 'Lucrezia', just like that and she whipped back her black hair like you see in the cartoons and he shot her right through her chest. She could have survived if the bullet hadn't splintered into her lungs, into everywhere really, and I was close by so I heard her die.

I went home and got some soda from the icebox. I like my soda so cold that my belly turns hard. I had the gun hidden in my room and as I sat there in the kitchen drinking my soda and watching Facebook, I thought of how Lucrezia had died looking at me. I don't believe in ghosts so I don't think she followed me home, but I felt she could have if there hadn't been so much blood.

My mother came home first. She put her briefcase so gently on the breakfast counter and she tried to smile but she couldn't. I knew she was looking at me as if I was an animal that had just leaped from a television nature programme. I opened my mouth and yawned. I imagined I had fangs.

My mother was trying to be nice. She poured me some milk since she knew I liked the taste of it and maybe she hoped deep down I hadn't changed so much, but I wanted to tell her that when you fix it for someone to die, and when you see it happening in front of you, something happens inside of you at the same time.

You can feel your heart squeezing out its feelings until there is nothing left.

Jones, that's the name of the boy that killed Lucrezia. Jones said I had a hard eye right in the middle of my forehead. He said he only saw boys like that, never girls, so I leaned over in his bed, took his cigarette and said, well now he's met a girl like me, and I was like something he had never met before.

I really liked the smile he gave me after I said that. He wasn't any Lucrezia but he was ok. He looked long and nice lying there on his bed. He said he had always liked guns.

His dad was making breakfast in the small kitchen down the corridor. He yelled up to us, 'how do you like your eggs?' then he giggled. He sounded sleazy but I didn't mind. My body was all warm and fuzzy from the toes up.

It hadn't been much with Jones, but the afterwards was cute. We nuzzled. His nose was a bit wet at times because he had a cold. He had kissed me right inside my mouth. His teeth had jammed against mine. He had got so hard inside me that I'd wondered – is this way it's done?

Jones's dad served us up pancakes as well. They were burnt on the edges but he squirted chocolate syrup all over mine.

'You look like a girl who needs feel good enzymes', he said.

I just said, 'thanks Mr Maddox'.

Jones and I walked back over the streets to my house. He snuggled into his jacket and he kicked leaves on the way. I walked tall. I was thinking of the gun.

I asked him, 'what's she like to kiss?'

Jones whipped his head round to look at me. 'Soft', he said. 'Like a pussycat, you know'. He licked his lips against the cold. 'She got all wiry on me', he said, 'like she wanted it then she didn't want it anymore. I told her to make up her mind then she slapped me'.

'You slapped her back, right?'

Jones laughed. 'Hell, no. I don't slap them. I love them'.

He sounded like his dad.

My Dad didn't like Jones. Neither did my mother. They watched him do homework with me, and even when Jones showed how good he was with co-ordinate geometry and logarithms, Dad wasn't all that impressed.

Instead he asked me, 'what happened to Lucrezia?'

Lucrezia originally came from Korea. She stood at the top of Mrs Allsop's class and she looked down through all of us from behind her glasses. Some boys snickered. I don't think Jones did. Jones was always quiet when he saw something interesting. Even grasshoppers interested Jones. He admired the hinges on their legs and the shine of their bug eyes.

I didn't love Lucrezia straight away. I didn't know if I even wanted to like her. She was smaller than me and she smelled of some kind of oil. Later she said it was coconut oil to keep her hair neat and behind her ears. Once I licked her hair without her knowing it. It was just a strand that had got caught in her desk. It swayed in the breeze made by everyone who walked by it. I wound it round my finger then I licked it.

'What happened to Lucrezia?' my Dad asked me.

I said I didn't know what happened to her.

She sat in front of me the first day and at recess some boy nudged her so hard her glasses fell. 'Slaphead', he called her. She blinked over at me but she didn't have any tears. I told her that Charlie Adams was a useless excuse for a human being as well as a racist and why didn't she have some of my Granola Bar with cherries in it?

It went on from there. I walked over to her house on a Saturday morning then we walked over to the community pool and played being fish for a while. She was a better swimmer. I just liked to see how the water ran drops on her arms and legs. She laughed when I belly-flopped. She laughed when I tried to beat her at length trials. She said my legs weren't made for duration. She pointed at my knees and said they were to blame. They were like big tight balls.

Like this, she said and she crunched her fist.

'Your knees don't allow the water to flow'.

I said, 'who died and made you Fu Man Choo?'

After that she refused to sit next to me at lunch break. She got different friends. I found her in the library and I asked her, why aren't we friends anymore. She put her glasses back on to look at me, and she said that I had a disturbing aspect to my personality. I said, don't you talk like you don't know me. Mr Georgis, the second library assistant told me that I was shouting when I said that. Mrs Allsop called my parents in and said my work had taken a major nosedive and she was worried about my emotional wellbeing.

In a way Jones happened to Lucrezia.

He hung around on the edges of her crowd and he laughed at her jokes. He listened to her stories about South Korea and how North Korea wanted it bombed out of existence. He said she was beautiful. I listened because he still talked to me at the school bus stop.

He said his dad was going to buy him a car for him to fix up. Jones wanted something to go fast with plenty of smoke. He blubbered his lips when he made the sound of a fast smoking car.

'Put Lucrezia in the front seat', he said, 'and ram right through to the highway'.

Someone told me that Lucrezia liked to slum. I don't remember who the someone was, just one of those blonde girls from her group, and she whispered it to me in the corridor, shoved up close so no one else would hear and she said, 'tell Jones he's just the slum picking of the week'.

I didn't tell Jones for three weeks. He highlighted his relationship status on his Facebook page. He didn't drop me but anything I posted didn't get so many likes. He told me that Lucrezia said that I was a sort of loner girl and if I got raped then she'd feel sorry for the rapist.

At home I ate my Mom's vegetarian dishes and I listened to her talk about yoga while my Dad pretended to listen and afterwards I hid in his study and I heard him talk soft and low on his cell phone to someone. He called her Suzanne. He made her sound precious. I went out to

Mom and watched her drink one glass of wine then she grabbed her car keys for the trip to her yoga class.

'You should finish the beetroot salad', she said. 'It'll give you colour'.

Lucrezia refused my Friend Request.

I drew a picture of her in my homework book. I concentrated on her hair. Someone found it and wrote on Mrs Allsop's blackboard.

Caitlin is a homo swine.

It was the swine bit that got me. I didn't mind the homo bit because it wasn't true and neither was the swine word either, but it got to me and so did the oink, oink noises that followed me in the corridors.

Then someone drew a pig with fat knees on Mrs Allsop's blackboard.

I threw up in the toilets but even then I didn't stop loving Lucrezia. I didn't stop loving her until she dumped Jones and his name went up on the Facebook post, *Slum Dump of The Week.*

So Jones and me started seeing more of each other after that and my Dad said, 'I don't want you spending time with that boy'.

I was eating food Mom had left in the refrigerator.

'I don't want you talking to Susanne anymore', I said.

Dad's face crumbled from the eyes down and I felt so glad inside that I had made him afraid of me and when Mom came home, Dad went into niceness overdrive. He talked about a vacation to anywhere, anywhere Mom and me liked.

I said nothing and I kept Dad's secret under my tongue like it was syrup.

My mother curled her fingers inside her hands while I drank my milk. It was so quiet I could hear her breathe. I could feel and hear everything I touched, the fake marble

Formica breakfast bar, even the sweat under my thighs as I sat on the stool, and the slow hum of the refrigerator made me think of Lucrezia lying on the ground.

Jones had said, 'wait till you see how she dies'.

She died funny. She died with her eyes wide open, and they were still moving as they looked at me, and blood came out her mouth, red but turning purple when it reached her blouse collar, then she tried to say something but then she stopped and I listened to her stop.

HUSK

I have written a number of letters to my brother. I have asked him to ask my husband to allow me home. The letters come back to me unopened, but I still go down to the privy, and I cough up bits of bread and blood and oatmeal and I press my womb against the privy wall because there cannot be a baby in me. My husband would not want a baby in me.

Mr Olson comes at night. He wears his moustache thick. His suit is yellow with brown threads. The Shit-Colour Man, old Katie calls him. She squats on her bed and squawks down, 'hey there Mr Shit-Colour Man, which one of us is for you tonight?'

Katie tells me she is fifty but she looks older. The food here is slowly killing her, she says. When she opens her mouth to laugh I can see where the tip of her tongue has been snipped into two pieces, like a snake's. Some men did that to her. They said she talked too much. They said they'd fix her tongue good.

Katie had a life before here. She lived in Morgantown and she had petticoats with tiny gold ribbons that her lover unloosed through his fingers.

I'm here my love, she croons to him in her sleep.

Mr Olson sits on my bed some nights. He says I'm a good woman. I don't believe him. If I was good or even if I pretended to be good, I would not be here. I would have my children. I would have my husband.

Mr Olson says my mind is like a dark room and he is just trying to light it up for me.

Katie says Mr Olson tells that story to everyone.

Mr Olson has three children. Sometimes they come to the asylum and look at us. They prefer the ones who are madder than I am. The ones who don't wash and the ones who scoot naked on the ground like monkeys, and trail their female blood so that Mr Olson's children giggle and dance.

Once I touched Mr Olson's youngest boy. He was barely six. When he looked at me, I thought his blue eyes turned like wheels inside his head. They had grey spokes. They turned and I screamed.

Men beat me after that.

Mr Olson told me to braid my hair. He said I looked neater that way. He meant saner. He told me to sit next to a window and read a book.

I read Washington Irving. Katie sat at my feet and chewed the hem of my new dress. Mr Olson appreciated this tableau. He said it had pathos and a shiver of gore. He approved of my reading material. I did not bother to remind him that he chose it for me as he had chosen my dress.

Mr Olson asked if I recognized the dress and I had to say that I did not.

'You were wearing it when you first arrived here, Florence'.

I studied the butterflies on the material. They had faded. They were old.

Brother, talk to my husband. Bring me home.

Katie is playing with spiders. She trails their webs through her tongue.

Mr Olson says, 'come now ladies, let us welcome our guests!'

The guests enter the room. I am sitting by the window, the book is in my hands. My old dress is too large and my breasts drop down inside it.

'The Legend of Sleepy Hollow', murmurs a man in a paisley cravat. He leans down close to my face and I marvel at the colours wrapped around his throat.

'Forty two', I hear Mr Olson say to a woman in a purple travelling coat. I can smell the outside air on her, the drench of autumn leaves.

'Ten years a patient', Mr Olsen is saying, 'but younger looking than when she was brought here. It's the air and the food we nourish them with'.

Katie grins up at me. She collects phlegm in her mouth then spits it at the lady in the purple coat. The lady squeals. The man with the cravat fingers my chin.

'Smooth skin', he murmurs.

He checks my eyes and presses around them.

'Good orbital depth', he says.

I glance at Mr Olson while the other man reaches in between the buttons of my gown. I close my eyes. My husband has thin hands. He ordered me to shut my womb after my second baby. He did not like my body. My hips were too wide. My babies dripped saliva like puppies and I went mad for a kind touch. I begged for love. I begged the bread boy once. His breath was full of stale yeast, and later when my husband learned from the cook of what I had done, he told my brother to find me another home.

'I must go home', I tell the man who is still rubbing his fingers on my skin inside my gown. 'I have children to feed'.

He is shocked at my voice, at my diction I would say.

'Educated', Mr Olson explains.

'And forgotten?' The visiting man enquires as he pulls away his fingers and wipes them with a handkerchief from his coat pocket.

Mr Olson answers, 'yes, forgotten. And now ...' He coughs into his hand. He coughs again.

'Aha', says the man in the paisley cravat.

That night, Mr Olson does not come to my bed but Katie does. She squats near my pillow. Her stink is warm. Other women chatter and cry in their beds. Some dig their hands in between their legs and move in the dark, mumbling their made-up love words.

'I know who he is', Katie whispers in my ear. Her eyes are big and cross-eyed this close to my face. 'He's the Mummy-Man'.

She holds up her hand in the dark.

'He keeps a dead man's hand under a glass case in his house'.

I laugh but I watch Katie's hand.

'And he invites people to dinner and gives them dead vegetables to eat!'

Katie nestles into me and goes to sleep but I lie awake. I press my womb down. Like a husk, I had promised my brother. Like a husk, I had pleaded as he carried me to this place. Like a husk, I had kissed him. I had clasped his shoulders, his arms and his waist until finally he was standing far away from me.

Mr Olson tells me that the gentleman with the paisley cravat is Mr Hamrick. He is a farmer and a part-time undertaker, and he has perfected mummification by using a recipe from the Bible. He and Mr Olson believe in scientific progress. Mr Hamrick will surpass the Egyptians.

Mr Olson presents me with a turnip. He says, 'Mr Hamrick makes an incision in the turnip, places it in an airtight box, and through a tube drains the vegetable of water. Through the same tube he injects saltpetre dissolved in water back into the vegetable. The fumes dry out the turnip perfectly, Florence'.

Over the next few days Mr Olsen shows me a 'pumpkin still bright and juicy from last year – the year of Our Lord 1886', also a collection of green apples and an orange from which he cuts one segment and eats it pith and skin. He peels another segment and my mouth waters.

I used to eat oranges so readily when I was a wife.

I bite in. There is juice but it is thin. It is like old water from a covered barrel.

Mr Olson stares at me. There is something he is not saying, but I can see it behind his eyes. When you are dead, Florence, when you are dead.

Mr Hamrick visits again. He brings cheap picture books of men fighting Algonquin Indians on the Virginia coastal plains. He tells me that Pocahontas was sold to the English for a copper kettle. He doesn't speak of what he has done with vegetables. He does not answer my questions about a preserved hand under a glass case, or of a man's head, or a dead but perfect baby lying in a blanketed cot.

Instead he watches how I move my face and he measures the length of my bones and the depth of my flesh. He listens to my lungs.

I tell him I want to go home. I tell him I have a husband. I show him how well I can write. How the words follow one another in the correct manner.

'Educated surely', Mr Hamrick admits.

Mr Olson denies me my pen. He says I am dying. He says my lungs are giving out. He still comes to my bed and settles himself inside my legs. He grunts and pushes. I close my eyes and I close my womb.

I cough up my food. I cough up my blood. I imagine that I am coughing up Mr Olson as well. I write my letters in my head. I write them every day. Husband, I will be good. Brother, come for me.

But Mr Hamrick is sitting in the corner of the room while I sit in a chair. He is telling me that he is an inventor and an experimenter. He is telling me I am someone he has chosen. He tells me all of this as if I am nothing more than a page he writes his words on.

He tells me that when I die, he will make my body live forever.

SOILED WELCOME

In Room 202, the walls keep talking to you.
I'll never tell you what they said.
So turn out the light and come to bed.
(anonymous American folksong)

Room 202 was situated on the second floor. It had one window that looked out over the tram junction and its glass windowpane reflected the shine from the THE WELCOME neon sign that the new would-be hotel owners had recently hitched onto the old masonry. They wanted to clean the place up. Jesús had told them often enough that wouldn't be possible. Life is too dirty here, he said. Too many ghosts as well. He smiled his broken teeth at his employers. They somehow liked him. He kept the place clean. He had a way with the room's inhabitants.

'Can't get rid of any of them even if they die', Jesús joked.

The new owners breakfasted every morning in the pseudo-Berlin-inspired and Berlin-titled café across the road while they observed their recent purchase through the current heatwave. They hadn't seen any ghosts yet. They had only noticed the present occupiers fluff out their clothes onto the street and water odd plants on their balconies. Since it had survived the 1906 earthquake the hotel's lobby was considered a monument to art deco, yet now only drug users, losers and ex-murderers inhabited it.

The owners wanted things to progress smoothly. They told their lawyer to be kind, or at least seem kind. They asked him to assist in persuading the younger hotel guests to leave, even if they had the beginnings of a family, surely it was better to live in the suburbs or a clean apartment elsewhere?

Jesús, the concierge leaned on his floor mop, and said, 'you pretty whites know nothing'.

The owners were convinced Jesús was a racist, but he was a darker colour than they and ideally they didn't want to say anything racist in return, so they smiled and said, 'but Jesús, this is our property now and surely it would be fairer to all concerned if *our guests* found other homes?'

'*Your guests*', Jesús said, '*have* homes'.

The male part of the new owner couple had certain ways of believing in things. He presumed he and the lawyer would see eye to eye. He assumed that the hotel guests would sit quietly during an appointed meeting in the old ballroom that until now did nothing but house old furniture and rotting refrigerators. He assumed that the audience would listen to him.

'They pay their rent', Jesús warned him. 'You can't get rid of them if they pay their rent'.

The female part of the new owner couple cried her eyes out at the philistine inhumanity before her but she believed in action. She picked out the more useable chairs. She ordered an emergency bulk of Febreze. She posted images on her Facebook page. She uploaded a Wordpress blog and she made sure she looked pretty in her surroundings of filth and questionable inhabitants.

She never called them anything other than '*our guests*'. The lawyer had final say on what his clients put on their social sites. He admired their gumption, their youth and sometimes he admired their stupidity.

He advised them against the meeting. He advised them first to call door to door to each hotel room. Be respectful, he said, especially to the older ones. There was an ex-soldier from Iraq, whom Jesús said was approachable only during the mornings on account of his hangover. It made him helpless and looking for his 'mommy'.

A young couple lived on the second floor. They liked the view, they had often confided to Jesús, and they were used to the traffic sounds, but all that was going to change if the new owners got their way, and also there was the sorry truth that their third child had fallen down the stairs some time ago, opening his head, and dying there. They could not and would not leave.

The meeting began so well that the hotel's new female owner distributed the finger food herself. The air smelled of roses and lemon Febreze. All the chairs were faced towards her husband who was standing on a makeshift podium. He was dressed down but his tie was last year's Tommy Hilfiger and because her husband looked so good now, she was going to eat him up later that night. Her husband sounded fine as he spoke about the intrinsic historical beauty and importance of the building. It was an original of 'Sixth Street'. A few mutters in the audience made him redirect his historical line. He wet his lips. He glanced at Jesús, who shrugged as if to say *this is your deal now*.

'But this is our home', one woman called up from the chairs. 'You can't throw us out. History or no history'.

The woman was old and covered in a number of dresses. The female hotel owner determined to be kind, to be understanding, sidled close to the woman, yet almost gagged from the other woman's urine odour.

'Would you care for a salmon bite?' she offered.

Looking at his wife down in the audience pit, her husband was glad he didn't actually have to touch any of them just yet. After his speech, he would shake hands or touch a child or two, although he was reluctant since the children seemed rabid with behaviour problems.

Jesús had said, 'you pretty whites have to treat us all with the same respect'.

His new boss tried to point out that the hotel's population percentage was predominantly white but he decided against that. Instead he gifted Jesús with a new TV for his office and a new MacBook for his reservation desk.

Jesús stood to the side of the podium and watched the tenants get angry.

Cal, the husband of the woman who had lost the baby, came up to Jesús. His wife stood further back with one of their other kids. Her name was Marmalade on account of her orange hair. It was one of those genetic links back to some Irish or Scottish grandfather. Her daughter had red hair also. She didn't speak much. Cal said it was trauma since she was the one who had pushed her brother down the stairs by mistake. Cal said now, 'you believe this crap, Jesús?'

'I'm just the concierge', Jesús answered.

Cal nodded at the woman handing out finger food.

'She can cook though'.

'It's catering', Jesús said. 'They want to sweeten you up'.

'I'm not leaving', Cal said. 'None of us are'. He sniffed and watched the woman swerve her tray of goodies. 'What's she like?'

Jesús curled his lips in over his teeth. 'She's got her standards', he replied.

He glanced around the old ballroom. It was still an impressive room. He knew that in the old days it had been hung with crystal chandeliers. During the 1906 earthquake those chandeliers had quivered, then smashed down on top of early morning cleaners from the night before, killing them, and later when they were finally unearthed from under the fallen tables and chairs, curtains and dust, Jesús had read somewhere that it was as if some butcher had wandered past and decided to try his knives on someone unsuspecting.

'Gwendolyn', Cal tried out. 'Gwen or Gwennie, which?'

Jesús was bored but asked, 'what?'

'Which one does he call her, her husband?'

Jesús trained his eye on the moving Gwendolyn Hazlitt. There was something about her eagerness to be liked, to be seen as harmless that held his imagination. He watched how she separated a few inches between her body and the tenants. He smiled and speculated, 'Gwen, when he wants to fuck her'.

The husband was called Magnus. The Hazlitt's had told Jesús that they were originally English from about three hundred years ago. There was a strain of them in Canada. They hoped that Jesús would stay on as the concierge.

Before the Hazlitt's arrival Jesús had got used to being the manager and the janitor. He sluiced down hallways of vomit and urine. He mopped the elevator's interior everyday because some of the female inhabitants entertained guests there. Jesús mopped up the smell of human sex so thoroughly that the old decorative ironwork held the permanent odour of bleach and Pine-Sol. Jesús liked the old building. He had even liked the 'For Sale' sign, badly positioned at the side of the defunct hotel and not too far above one of the dumpsters. The city finally wanted to get rid of it but only as a going concern. It was one of those new initiatives that Jesús had read about. Get perky, solvent would-be successful business people to show off their creativity and sass, while elevating the living standards of the poor.

Cal's wife ambled up. 'Hey', she said to Jesús.

Jesús nodded but turned his attention to Magnus Hazlitt still on his high-horse, but redder in the face because the Iraqi war vet had stood up and begun to yell that he loved his bed and he wasn't going to change it for some butter-fed boy and his bitch.

Everyone laughed. Even Jesús, but Gwendolyn Hazlitt caught his eye, her little mouth open in astonishment and hurt. Jesús went up to her. First of all he glanced at the salmon biscuits on her plate. He could see yellow oil on the salad leaves. It gave him a second to think. 'You've got to understand, Ms Hazlitt. He's mad and he's scared'.

He called her Ms Hazlitt because he knew she liked that. The first time he had seen her she had waltzed in with her husband, dressed against the heat and looking cool. Her hair was all tied up on top, then let fall down in frizzled tendrils. Jesús knew how her hair would feel between his fingers. She was fanning her face with a vendor's brochure. He took one look at her, then another look at her husband and he knew the hotel would be theirs.

'I keep the place clean', Jesús had assured them and she had turned her bright smile on him so his bones went warm.

'We want someone like you', she said, 'don't we Magnus?'

Eager to please and we mean you no harm. It took Jesús only seconds to gauge how to treat these people. He stared at the space between them, then stepped into it first. There was a sigh of relief from the couple. They handed over their hands, their politeness, their willingness to be fair and their complete assumption that Jesús understood their predicament, that Jesús would be a loyal, invaluable employee and an ally.

But the meeting had not been a good move.

After the 'butter boy and his bitch' statement and despite Jesús's explanation to Gwendolyn Hazlitt, some kid threw a used panty-liner at Magnus Hazlitt's head. It hit his cheek and there was a flash aroma of vaginal blood before the panty-liner fell to lie face-up at Magnus's feet. The vaginal blood was almost fresh. His stomach sawed and he opened his mouth, but at the back of his head was a small and cautioning voice – don't rile the enemy, don't rile the rats.

The audience roared into laughter. Even Marmalade smiled. She put her hand down on her youngest child's head, her remaining son. She thought of the neat pile of clean panty-liners in her underwear drawer. She tugged her son's ears and he snuggled close.

Marmalade's daughter was in front of the podium, her right arm easing down from an arc throw.

Cal went through the crowd fast. A few arms grabbed him on the way. A woman kissed his face, whispered into his ear, 'what a little doll she is, what a little angel'.

A tobacco-flavoured kiss on his mouth, a nudge to his gut, a pat on his shoulder and finally his own daughter nestling into him, her elbows jutting out so he could hold her safe from the man standing above her.

Magnus Hazlitt had taken classes on crowd psychology. Magnus Hazlitt was proud of what he was capable of achieving. He just needed to see the battle terrain and now it seethed in front of him and the enemy was waiting for the exact excuse to tear him and his dreams down.

Magnus did not wipe his face. He didn't even kick the used panty-liner away from his polished shoe. He eased his spit up to his back teeth. He swallowed his crawling contempt, and he smiled at the man that was holding onto the girl.

'What's her name?' he asked.

Cal had to think, then he answered, 'Juniper … June for short'.

Magnus lowered himself to just above the girl's face. Her eyes scared him a little. They were x-ray eyes. He could see the tiny lines of hazel at her pupil and the flash-lines of the yellow and brown of her iris.

'June', he said to begin with.

The girl's mouth went straight.

'Juniper', Magnus corrected.

She put her head back against her father's torso. She wasn't a bad looking kid and if memory served Magnus as it usually did, then this was the girl who had inadvertently killed her own brother.

Magnus smiled. He said, 'let's just forget about this, ok?'

'Yeah, ok', said her father.

Magnus stood up and surveyed the room. He saw Jesús was standing just behind Gwendolyn. Everyone was waiting for something. Magnus shuttled his tie-knot tight into his collar. He held his hands up. He proclaimed, 'you know, I wanted things to be smoother today. I thought this was the fairest way and let's face it the more time-economical way of dealing with reality here'. He paused. He saw Jesús walk to the back of the ballroom, then halt at the entrance. 'But I was wrong. I'll do it differently. I promise'.

'You can't get rid of us', someone called out.

Magnus didn't look at who that was, and instead he focussed a smile on his wife. She was still standing there with that damn platter of food that none of the hotel's freeloaders had hardly known existed except on TV.

Magnus glanced up at the walls of the ballroom. It was a good space for conferences, weddings, and dinner-dances. He imagined the people he wanted here. He imagined the décor. There was the period detail to be considered but Magnus had this idea of his modern world, his clean world replacing the old from the inside out. State of the art wiring, discreet cameras, WiFi in each of the rooms, well-appointed reproduction furniture, and Gwendolyn, his Gwen, his PR genius, who had sided with him on the meeting idea against their lawyer's advice – she would have to up her game, she would have to deploy major damage control via her social media outlets.

'You won't get rid of us', someone shouted.

'Rent control', another voice yelled. Then more voices. 'Rent control, rent control, rent control'.

Rat control, Magnus thought. He stepped off his podium and brushed past Juniper and her father. He saw Gwendolyn deposit her food platter on a nearby empty seat. She was flustered but halfway smiling. She kissed and bit his ear as he drew level.

'Imagine', she whispered into it. 'Your bitch'.

Later that night she wrote the day down in her blog. The ballroom meeting, the bodily smell of the people, their smiles of hate, the pink salmon meat turning brown on its biscuit, her own desperation smelling like sweat as she had moved and greeted all these people she had never really wanted to know, but she was there because of her husband's dream to be a man of real property, to shake up the dregs and create something marvellous – something she wanted to believe in – and despite the photographic image of Marmalade's bloodied panty-liner, despite the smell of the place and the walls that peered down on her, despite the fact that she was afraid for the first time in her life, afraid of people different to her, she still wanted to believe in her husband and believe in the good he and she could bring to the community.

She titled it and pressed *Publish*.

In the Berlin café eating peach strudel Magnus and Gwendolyn Hazlitt considered their plan of attack. According to the lawyer, they had two options still worth considering. Sell it or live with it.

Gwendolyn played with the thick orange-coloured filling. She was nervous and whenever she glanced up through the rain-wet window, she disliked the neon THE WELCOME sign more and more.

'It's crude', she told Magnus.

The sign blinked its colour changes at her. Magnus's idea. He had seen something similar on a hotel in Northern Europe, and it mimicked the Northern Lights. The colours went from lavender to strong green, from boiling red to an opal-white and now as she gazed at it, it changed into a dark orange which had lit up the right-hand side window panel of a room on the second floor.

'Who is in that room?' she said.

Her husband looked up from his legal papers. He barely saw the window.

'I don't know'.

'Somebody must be in that room'.

Magnus blinked at her. *Quiet*, his blink said. *Quiet*.

'Well, we'll visit it, won't we?' She insisted. 'Jesús can introduce us'.

Magnus stared out at the hotel. He had ordered that sign. He had watched it go up. He had wanted to bring in industrial cleaners, man and machine. Jesús had said the dirt wouldn't go no matter what Magnus did. The lawyer had said, you own the building but you've got live-in tenants. Sell them or live with them.

The dirt, Magnus considered.

'Rats', he said out loud.

Gwendolyn paused over her coffee cup.

'Real ones', he said. 'Live bastards that will infest the place'. He sat back in his chair and grinned. 'Health and Safety. Have the building condemned for those reasons and abracadabra!'

'They already have rats', Gwendolyn said. 'Jesús traps them'.

'Mess up the wiring', Magnus suggested.

'What if somebody gets electrocuted, Magnus?'

He stared at her. 'Aren't you supposed to be on my side?'

'Yes'.

'Well, don't you think you should pay attention to my ideas?'

They began with the war vet on the fourth floor. Here the décor was more modern, circa the seventies. Plain walls with plain grey wash. It had a broken water fountain situated at the top of the staircase. Jesús said it had stopped dispensing water fifteen years ago.

'That's how long you've been here, Jesús?' Gwendolyn asked.

He answered, 'add ten more'.

She looked at his face. He didn't look that old. She and Magnus stood back and let Jesús knock.

Before it was answered, Magnus asked Jesús, 'what's his politics?'

Jesús shrugged. Another door further on down the corridor opened and a girl's head popped out, pissed off with what she saw.

'Herbert's not awake yet'. She aimed for Jesus. 'Are you coming this way?'

He nodded at her.

'Make me the last. I'm busy sleeping'.

'A working girl', Magnus surmised once the girl had shut her door. Jesús glanced at his male employer's tight face, then at Gwendolyn's pale, juicy cream-coloured skin.

Herbert's door opened.

'Mr and Mrs Hazlitt', Jesús announced.

Herbert's room was shuttered down against the morning light and it smelled of unwashed man and unwashed beer and disused pizza trays.

Herbert was careful to be neighbourly. He offered coffee. Gwendolyn said yes. Magnus said no, and Jesús wandered to the kitchenette to switch on Herbert's coffee pot. He searched for a delicate cup and found one – a blue design of Chinese women crossing a hump-backed bridge. The coffee boiled thick in its glass jug. It smelled burnt but Gwendolyn drank it all the same, saying thank you to Jesús after her first sip.

Magnus was trying to get Herbert to see sense. He asked about family.

'None'.

'None alive or none talking to you?'

Herbert stared at the boy in the pale grey suit who was sweating in the heat, licking his top lip and sometimes licking the bottom edges of his queer moustache.

'None', he answered.

'Don't you want a real home?' Magnus insisted. 'Doesn't the government or the military take care of men like you? Men who served, men who fought for our freedom and our standing in this world?'

Herbert cracked a laugh. He cracked it so hard he began to cough. Sputum dribbled down his chin and Gwendolyn pulled her toes further back within her high-heeled sandals.

Magnus smiled hard. Herbert grinned back.

'That little girl has a sweet throw', he said.

There was quiet in the room. Jesús watched Gwendolyn drink her coffee. He wondered if she would look up at him and she did. There was nothing too sexual in her look but it was nice.

Magnus said, 'sooner or later we are going to re-establish this hotel, Herbert'.

Herbert lifted his eyebrows. 'Tell him how long I've lived here, Jesús'.

'Twelve years'.

'I'm not moving, Butter-Boy'.

The next room housed a mother and her forty-year old son. They didn't like visitors, Jesús had explained. The son was a drug dealer. The mother fed him fish on Fridays religiously, and she made him put plastic over his sheets whenever a girl stayed over. The mother sat in the small kitchen while her son asked how much would Magnus pay them to leave.

'If you pay us five years worth of double rent plus some on top, we'll think about it'.

In the next room the working girl sat on her windowsill while she painted her toes.

She smiled through Gwendolyn and said, 'I read your blog'.

She lit a cigarette, clamped it between her teeth, and ran her hand-held fan over her varnished nails, looked at Gwendolyn then back to Jesus.

'That white bitch has a way with words'.

Her voice was so soft even the word bitch sounded agreeable to Gwendolyn.

Room 301 housed an ex-murderer. He seemed likeable to Magnus, almost white collar in appearance. He offered sparkling water. He said he had enjoyed the salmon bits at the meeting the previous day.

'And what was that cake?' he asked Gwendolyn.

'French chocolate'.

The ex-murderer's name was Preston James.

He showed the Hazlitts his book of cuttings. His crimes had been reported over a period of ten years. He was fully rehabilitated now. He understood the value of life and he had found Jesus the Christ, not Jesús the janitor.

Jesús laughed. He was used to the joke.

'But I can't move from here', Preston James said. 'Jesus won't follow me if I move'.

In 204 Marmalade was preparing meat stew for her family.

She glanced back through the beaded doorway and into her small living room.

'He won't apologise for her', she said. 'And I won't either'.

Marmalade's daughter was sitting in the living room watching TV. She had not said hello. She had not said anything. Gwendolyn had used the best smile she could have used in the circumstances, but the girl had just stared at her once then ignored her.

'I read your blog', Marmalade said. The meat spat in the hot oil. '*Soiled Welcome*? You think you're something different, don't you?'

'No', Gwendolyn lied.

Marmalade laughed and reached over for salt. 'Jesús said you looked like an angel the first time he saw you'. She leaned back from her gas ring to look at Gwendolyn's husband through the beads.

'You going to have any children?'

'Not yet', Gwendolyn answered.

Marmalade held up her meat spoon. 'I wanted one. Then I wanted two, and Cal liked me round, you know … *Hmmm* he used to whisper into my belly. Yours ever do that for you?'

'Sometimes', Gwendolyn lied.

'Then I had three. The third is dead'.

'I'm sorry'.

'So you see, I'm not leaving. Cal can leave. They all can leave but not me. Because I go down those stairs and when I hear my tiny boy playing I sit on those stairs and I talk to him'.

'But there are no such things as ghosts', Gwendolyn suggested.

Marmalade lowered her face close to the hot sputtering oil.

'I see him', she said. 'And I talk to him'.

The lawyer met the Hazlitts in the Berlin Café for an evening drink. He said Gwendolyn's damn blog post had gone viral. He said in his opinion the subtext was not only racist but elitist as well. His own reputation was on the line.

'I'm not a racist', Gwendolyn said.

'Yes you are', Magnus told her. 'We all are'.

He watched his wife play with her wine glass. He stared right through her head to the wall beyond her. He thought, *if I didn't have her ... if I was on my own.*

'Delete the blog and shut down your Facebook account', their lawyer advised. He rubbed his spectacles with the table napkin and yawned. He was tired of twenty-first century yuppies. Tired of their retro-charm and their do-gooder faces. The Hazlitts were old money made good again, old money made essential because of the recession, and now old money made even more stupid because of good old greed.

'What made you do it?' he asked them.

He didn't just mean the blog post. He meant the hotel. He meant the meeting. He meant the soft-soaping of Jesús. He was a lawyer and he could see Jesús. He could see Jesús see Gwendolyn. The lawyer could have laughed.

He could have laughed in their dumb faces.

'I'm not a racist', Gwendolyn insisted.

She waited for her husband to defend her, and because he didn't, she stared down at the remains of her cherry cheesecake. None of this had been her dream. Marriage had been her dream. She thought of Marmalade standing at her greasy oven, sweating in the heat, sipping water and stirring that damn meat stew.

She glanced out through the café's window. Room 202's window was now open. She had opened it. She had leaned out on her elbows and breathed in the street's exhaust fumes and behind her somebody had moved so softly it was almost as if he were a ghost which had peeled itself from any of the room's walls.

'I'm not a racist', she said again.

'*Soiled Welcome*', the lawyer said. '*Soiled*?'

It was if he held the bloodied panty-liner in front of her nose.

But her husband ordered another round of beer to keep the lawyer sweet, then he angled his right shoulder into Gwendolyn's face. *Shut up*, it said to her. *Shut up*.

She stared at her husband's shoulder. She laughed to herself, then said out loud, 'your penis never says anything to me, Magnus'.

Magnus turned. 'What?'

'Your penis never says anything anymore, Magnus'.

Gwendolyn cut a little of her cheesecake and placed it on her tongue. For a red-mad second Magnus wanted to crush her mouth.

The lawyer stepped in and said, 'just get rid of the blog, Gwendolyn'.

Gwendolyn stared at his face. It was calm, grey and un-sweating, so she decided to confess to him instead.

'I was in Room 202'.

She had left Marmalade's kitchen, and walked through her stuffy living area, and had been briefly caught by her husband's arm and Cal's wide smile.

'Mrs H', Cal called her.

Her husband pinched her to a near halt. 'Gwendolyn?'

'I need air', she had told him.

Marmalade's daughter came after her into the corridor. She stared at Gwendolyn.

'You sick?'

'No'.

The girl walked to the very edge of the staircase and pointed. 'I threw him down there'.

'Did you?'

'I didn't mean it, but I did it', the girl said.

Gwendolyn nodded. The girl looked about thirteen. Narrow legs and narrow arms and now she rested her whole body against the wooden rail, pressing hard, leaning back, then throwing herself harder against the wood, smiling down at the floor far below.

'Careful', Gwendolyn knew she should say but she didn't.

'I sometimes play with him', the girl called after her.

Gwendolyn stood outside Room 202.

'You going in there?' the girl called.

Gwendolyn entered the room. There was a bed situated close to a bathroom door and to the right of where she stood there was a tiny kitchenette. It was similar to Herbert's room in layout. There was no TV. There were no drapes on the window. There was a walled-up fireplace and a small couch facing it.

The bed sheets were straight and tight.

Jesús followed her inside and shut the door. Gwendolyn heard the lock click as if it were her own body clicking into somewhere safe.

She sat on the bed and closed her eyes. She eased off her shoes and pressed her heels into the cold rough carpet. She smelled dust in the air. Jesús kissed her and his broken teeth lodged just inside her lips and from the corner of her eye she imagined that she saw the wall move out of itself as if there was someone slipping into the room to watch.

She laughed into Jesús's mouth.

Welcome.